Maeve's Book of Beasts

The DragonFate Novels #1

DEBORAH COOKE

Books by Deborah Cooke

Paranormal Romance

The Dragonfire Novels
Kiss of Fire
Kiss of Fury
Kiss of Fate
Winter Kiss
Harmonia's Kiss
Whisper Kiss
Darkfire Kiss
Flashfire
Ember's Kiss
Kiss of Danger
Kiss of Darkness
Kiss of Destiny
Serpent's Kiss
Firestorm Forever

The Dragons of Incendium:
Wyvern's Mate
Nero's Dream
Wyvern's Prince
Arista's Legacy
Wyvern's Warrior
Kraw's Secret
Wyvern's Outlaw
Celo's Quest
Wyvern's Angel
Nimue's Gift

The DragonFate Novels
Maeve's Book of Beasts
Dragon's Kiss

Dragon's Heart
Dragon's Mate (2020)

The Prometheus Project
Fallen
Guardian
Rebel
Abyss

SHORT WORKS
An Elegy for Melusine
Coven of Mercy

For information about Deborah Cooke contemporary
romances, please visit:

HTTP://DEBORAHCOOKE.COM

For information about Claire Delacroix historical
romances, please visit:

HTTP://DELACROIX.NET

PROLOGUE

Manhattan—Saturday, October 26, 2019

el came home late, as usual, and exhausted, as usual. Though she thought of it as late Friday night, it was actually early Saturday morning. The street outside her building was deserted, the shadows dark. It had rained all day and the streets were slick with water. The air was damp and she hoped the boiler had been turned on for the building. Her landlord was cheap, though, and might hold out until the first of November.

A hot bath might have to do it. Her feet were sore and her back ached; the staircase seemed both steeper and longer than usual. Waiting tables was the hardest work she'd done in all her centuries and in just twelve short hours, she'd get to do it all over again.

Sooner or later, Mel had to catch a break.

The red string knotted around her left wrist burned like a bitch, the way it always did when she was feeling more mortal than would be ideal.

Maybe the guy who rented the place at the end of the hall would be awake. She guessed that he'd be watching, if so. That was his best, and maybe his only, trick. She didn't even know if the Watcher was a guy. She'd never even seen him—she just felt his presence when she went down the hall to her teeny apartment, a hot gaze boring into her back. She'd knocked on the door to challenge him once, but no one had answered.

She thought something had flashed behind the peep hole.

She'd heard him breathing and it had creeped her out—which was saying something, given her own credentials.

The Watcher had to be a guy. Watching seemed like a more masculine hobby to her. More importantly, anyone who watched her was either an enemy or a potential ally. There was no middle ground. If the Watcher was against her, she'd rather know soon.

Mel felt Raymond's ghostly presence behind her but ignored her dead ex with practiced ease. It was only when he began to complain that she addressed him. "Ghosts don't get tired," she muttered.

"Do not take a wager on that, my lady," he replied, still as courtly in his manners as he had been nine centuries before.

Mel just rolled her eyes.

Her studio apartment was on the top floor of the old apartment building, one that was in pretty bad shape. It was in a crappy neighborhood, not far from either the docks or even crappier areas. There was another unit on the top floor, its door opposite her own, but she'd never seen inside.

That was where the Watcher lived.

She'd only rented this place because Raymond had heard a rumor from his fellow ghosts that it contained a portal, exactly the kind of portal she'd been seeking. All she wanted was to sneak into the realm of the Fae, without Maeve knowing. Mel knew lots of official portals, but they were all watched by Maeve's allies. She'd been summoned by Maeve, too, more than enough times for her taste. If she was going to escape Maeve's grip, she had to be stealthy.

Three months and a whole lot of stairs later, Mel was ready to admit that the apartment had been yet another dead end. The only thing it opened onto was a lousy view.

The dead had lied to her—or to Raymond—one more time.

They were tiresome like that.

Time to move on. Time to find another lead. Time to try another angle. Over and over and over again, through all eternity. If Mel was honest with herself—and she frequently was—she'd admit it wasn't the long hours that wore her out. She was half-Fae. She didn't need much R&R. It was the growing sense of futility that was grinding her down.

The prospect of being trapped like this forever wore her out.

Just the way the bitch had planned it.

All Mel wanted was for her luck to change. She could catch one break after nine hundred years of zero progress.

She unlocked the door of her apartment and froze on the threshold. Something was wrong. She felt it before she saw it. A tingle ran over her flesh, leaving goosebumps behind.

The light of the moon slanted silver through the skylight overhead, illuminating the corpse sprawled on her floor.

There was a naked dead guy in her apartment.

He hadn't been there when she'd left.

She would have noticed.

Mel's luck *had* just changed, and not for the better.

Raymond slipped past her, and she felt a slight chill at his passing. He was curious about a new companion, no doubt.

Mel's eyes narrowed as a wisp of black smoke rose from the corpse and disappeared right before her eyes. Even Raymond turned to watch it.

It looked like a black feather.

Oh no.

Maybe the dead guy was just a vision, she told herself. A portent.

She crossed the floor and crouched down beside him. He looked pretty substantial for a vision. He was as muscled as a bodybuilder, a big buff guy. Naked, as she'd noticed already. There was an enormous dark pool beneath him and she could smell the blood. He was on his chest, feet closest to her, as if he'd fallen on his face. There was an arrow shaft buried in his back and the blood flowed from that wound.

There were also two long scars on his back, like a V that didn't join at the bottom.

Mel swallowed when she saw them. The skylight wasn't broken. The door had still been locked. The windows were secured, but there was a dead fallen angel in her apartment even so.

The apartment *was* a portal.

But Mel was too late to learn anything from this guest.

Or maybe not. She stepped forward when she noticed the book in his hand. It was flickering, caught between the realms. Raymond fussed—he'd become such a chicken shit since he'd died, which on better days, she thought was funny—as Mel seized the book and eased it from the dead angel's slack grasp.

His body shimmered then, as if it was made of dark starlight. She stared, then caught her breath when he disappeared as if he had never been. Even the spilled blood on the floor was gone, but the apartment remained icy cold.

All that was left was a triangle of sharpened

stone.

The head from the Fae arrow that had killed him.

"Probably poisoned," Raymond whispered as Mel reached for it. "You know how thorough she is."

She got a plastic bag from the kitchen and picked up the arrow head, distrusted how it shimmered in her hand. But it had to be of this realm, because it had remained behind. The Fae liked quartz, because it took a magickal charge, she remembered. The stone might have been granite, with quartz crystals in it. She sealed the bag and tucked it into her pocket, out of sight, and considered the book.

It felt solid in her hands and she held it tightly, not trusting it to remain in the mortal realm. It was old and leatherbound, and the cover creaked when she opened it. She could see that the pages were thick and a quick sniff told her that they were vellum. Why did a fallen angel have an antique book in his possession? Was it why he'd been killed?

Why had he brought it to her apartment? That had to be important.

Mel angled the cover toward the moonlight, halfway thinking she could see a title, then shivered when she read it.

Maeve's Book of Beasts.

Holy shit. She almost dropped the book.

What had this angel done?

In a way, she was no longer surprised that he'd

been shot dead.

"I'll take that," said a man from behind her, his tone both deep and officious. Mel spun, clutching the book to her chest, recalling a bit late that she'd left the door open. He had an accent, maybe French, and was tall with broad shoulders. He moved into her apartment with a fluid grace that was familiar in an unwelcome way. His blue eyes gleamed with intent and the hand he extended was pale.

Please, not a vampire. Mel could deal with any of the Others, but she hated vampires.

Vampires did not play for the team, no matter what the stakes.

"I'll take it now," he said, his voice dropping deeper as he proved her assumption true, and she glimpsed the points of his teeth.

"You're the Watcher," she said. "From the other apartment."

"What matters is that book," he said with impatience. "I've been waiting for it."

"Then you should have had your courier bring it to your apartment."

"Accuracy is difficult for most beings under duress," he snapped. "And the portal is here."

"Finders keepers," Mel said.

His eyes flashed. "Give it to me before she has another reason to curse you."

Mel felt a flicker of panic, but he couldn't know who she really was.

"Oh, but I do," he murmured, as if he had read

her thoughts. Did he have Maeve's power to discern any secret?

"No," he said softly and smiled coldly at her surprise. "But I find the thinking of humans and Others to be painfully obvious." His hand landed on the book. He tugged and she had a sudden sense of his power—and his determination.

Vampires had incredible strength. He would tear it from her grip easily, if she didn't surrender it willingly. She tightened her grip upon it, intending to defend it to her last.

"Your death can be arranged, Melusine de Lusignan, and very easily," he hissed. "But I think you will find it preferable to give me the book."

"Who are you?"

"You can call me Sebastian, if you must."

"What are you going to do with it?"

"Defend it far better than you can. She will demand its return. She will hunt it down. I would not want to be the one holding it when she comes through the portal after her prize."

The air shimmered behind Mel as if the dark queen was coming through the portal that very moment. Mel had no interest in seeing that monarch any sooner than was absolutely necessary.

"But we need it," she protested. "We need to work together to defeat her and we can use it to find all of the Others."

Sebastian's expression turned mocking. "We?"

"The Others. We're joining forces."

"So I've heard." His disinterest was clear.

"If you have a plan for the book, you have to share it. We have to be a part of the solution. We all have so much to lose."

Sebastian's lips thinned and Mel knew he was going to snatch the book and disregard her plea. Raymond started, though, and looked toward the door. She could almost make out the silhouette of another man there.

"We will join the Others," he said and Sebastian inhaled sharply. "It has been decided."

Sebastian spun and glared at the other vampire. "You mean you have decided. I didn't join your little group to lose all autonomy."

"No, you joined to survive."

"The more who are involved, the greater the risk of failure," Sebastian snapped. "We've gotten this far because of trust and silence."

"And we will go further with the Others," that vampire said, no heat in his tone. "I am Micah, of the Coven of Mercy," he said and Mel knew the introduction was addressed to her. "We have a plan for the book, one that should see the dark queen defeated."

"I'm all ears," Mel said.

"There is no time to explain," Micah said mildly. He was remarkably serene for a vampire. In Mel's experience, they tended to be more volatile, like Sebastian. "And all is already in motion. That is why he stole the book."

"You have to share the plan," Mel said. Vampires and their mysteries. Everything would be so much simpler if they didn't feel compelled to keep secrets.

"You can't compromise what's been accomplished," Sebastian protested.

Micah inclined his head. "I will make a concession as a sign of goodwill. We will launch the plan in the location of your choice."

Sebastian hissed disapproval. "We'll lose it all," he muttered, but Micah ignored him.

"Bones," Mel said immediately, naming the bar where she worked and the refuge of the Others. She would have back-up there, and more allies.

"Bones," Micah agreed. "Tomorrow night."

"The problem with all of you is that you have no respect for magick." Sebastian plucked the book from Mel's hands. "I'd think that you, of all Others, would be smarter than that," he said to Mel. The vampire retreated with astonishing speed: one minute he was right before her, claiming the book, and the next, she was alone with Raymond as the other apartment door closed with a click. She looked down the hall but couldn't see even a shadowy hint of Micah's presence, and didn't feel anyone watching her.

But there was something behind her. The air was rippling and shimmering again, and Raymond backed away from the disruption warily. When the whorling red and black appeared in the air, Mel swallowed. She knew where this portal would take her—and that she had no choice but to obey.

"She's summoning you," Raymond whispered.

"I'll go alone," she whispered back. "It'll be fine."

Raymond moaned. He hated the Fae realm and he hated being separated from Mel. His fear of Maeve trumped all, though, and he cowered in a corner, trying to make himself invisible as the red and black light began to pulse.

Mel knew she would be interrogated, perhaps by the dark queen herself. She'd want that book back. And even though Sebastian was a reluctant ally, Mel wouldn't betray him or Micah. She pushed their images and names from her thoughts, as well as her recollection of everything that had happened since she climbed the stairs to her apartment. She gave the memory to Raymond for safekeeping, then voided it from her own mind.

She could only hope it would be enough.

CHAPTER ONE

*B*ones.

Not a really promising name for a restaurant, in Sylvia's opinion. The area was skeevy, too, and she'd been looking over her shoulder for the last four blocks.

Emily, characteristically, was undeterred. She marched right in the door of the restaurant—which was blacked out and had a security grill that could be locked over it when closed—and took a deep breath.

"Oh yeah." Emily smiled, apparently unaware of how odd the place was. The restaurant was in a converted warehouse in a zone near the docks that hadn't yet been gentrified. It had a bit of edge as a result. They'd stepped around street pizza on their way in, and passed a lot of gang tags on the walls. Sylvia had made a mental note to head home early.

"When I wished for my life to get more interesting, I wasn't hoping to be mugged and left for dead in an alley," Sylvia complained.

"Which shows a real lack of adventure on your part," Emily said with a grin. She shook a finger at Sylvia and opened the door. "Root of the issue, I think."

"There are lots of restaurants serving pulled pork closer to my place. Much nicer restaurants in much safer neighborhoods."

"But you only live once, Syl, and this place is supposed to be the best."

The interior space was huge, and so dark that Sylvia knew she couldn't see it all. How high did the ceiling go? It was lost in shadows. There was an exposed brick wall on the other side of the bar, and the windows were all glass blocks. That gave the place an industrial air, but probably was more secure. The bar was in the middle of the space, a big open rectangle that was a natural focus. The counters on each side were long and black, polished to a shine, with stools on the outside perimeter. There was an island in the middle, stacked with all kinds of liquor, and glasses hung from racks over the bartenders' head. Sylvia guessed that they could have four or five bartenders easily working in that space, although there was only one at the moment. She was tiny, with dark hair, thick eyeliner and a lot of silver jewelry.

Every table was empty. Empty restaurants at meal time were never a good thing. It was Thursday night at seven. They shouldn't have been the only customers.

Emily waved to the cluster of staff at the bar, who seemed unaware of their arrival. "Hey there!"

The three waitresses and bartender turned to look at them, as if they were surprised by the presence of the two women.

It wasn't *that* early.

"Are you sure this is the right place?" Sylvia asked in an undertone. It wouldn't have been the first time that Emily had led them astray with her online research. "We could go somewhere else."

"Why? It's got great ambiance, and the food smells really good." Emily tapped on her phone, pulling up the listing. *"Bones offers a unique ambiance in an unexpected neighborhood and the best pulled-pork barbeque in Manhattan. A hidden gem. Three forks. No reservations required.* Sounds good to me. Do you know how long it's been since I had some really rocking barbeque?"

"The people look a little weird."

Emily gave Sylvia a despairing look. "Please. This is Manhattan. Weird comes with the territory."

"Not usually this weird. I know from weird. I live here."

"You don't live around here. It said 'unique ambiance'. Yoo hoo!" Emily waved again, as no one had moved closer. "If you're over the big city, Syl, you can always come back to Podunk Junction with me in the morning."

"Don't make fun of your small town. That's not even what it's called. And you love it there."

"I do, but only because I'm there with Mike, my hot gingerbear heart-throb. If I was looking for a man there, I'd come screaming back downtown in a heartbeat." Emily smiled at the approaching hostess. "For two, please."

The hostess was in Goth gear, as if it was still the mid-eighties, and had a lot of tattoos. Her skirt was black leather and very short. Her stockings were torn fishnets, and her eyeliner was the thickest Sylvia had seen in a while. She was wearing a Ramones T-shirt, torn and embellished with safety pins. What was really strange was the cloud that followed her, the one that seemed to be filled with seething black snakes. That was definitely unusual.

Sylvia blinked and it disappeared.

She really needed something to eat. She was starting to see things.

The hostess showed them to a booth and left them with menus, never saying a word. Sylvia watched her retreat, looking for the snakes, but to her relief they were gone.

Emily picked up the menu. "I'm starving," she whispered, running a finger down the list of offerings.

Sylvia knew from experience that Emily would order enough for both of them.

"Wine?" she asked, hoping.

"Beer," Emily said flatly. "You have to have beer

with barbeque. Or tequila."

"I'd rather have wine."

"You'd rather have a grilled chicken breast with steamed veggies, too, but you lose. It's your birthday and my treat." She gave Sylvia an intent look. "This is part of the grand adventure, which you wished for. Life gets more interesting right now."

"I could wait until tomorrow."

"I'm only here now, and I have to work with opportunity. There will be no vegetables tonight, unless they're battered and deep-fried."

"Why do I have the sense that you'll fight me even on that?"

"Because you know me so well." Emily smiled. "And to know me is to love me." She waved a hand. "And to eat barbeque and battered fries with me is the dream of every sentient being. Trust me on that."

Sylvia smiled. Emily was enjoying the menu so much that she looked around again, leaving the choices to her friend.

They definitely had crossed to the wrong side of the tracks, and probably looked completely out of place. She was wearing black, but her jacket and skirt were sleek separates. Emily, of course, was wearing purple from head to toe, and had even put a bit of purple dye in her hair since the last time they'd seen each other. She might as well have been wearing a neon sign that said *Visiting from the 'Burbs.*

Or Podunk Junction.

But Sylvia's sense of danger came from more

than the neighborhood. There was a haze in the air and she felt a weird prickling at the back of her neck, as if lightning was going to strike. She wondered if the wiring was up to code.

One thing was for sure—she'd avoid any armwrestling contests with either of the waitresses. They were tough-looking chicks, with copious tattoos. Maybe she and Emily didn't look like they belonged because they had no ink.

A burly guy had appeared and was talking to the bartender, apparently giving instructions. He could have been the leader of a biker gang. He was stocky and short, and spoke gruffly to the tiny dark-haired bartender. Sylvia squinted, seeing something green floating over her head. It looked almost like a miniature dragon, but that would have been nuts.

Again, she blinked and it vanished.

Come to think of it, one of the waitresses had one, too. Hers looked like a black bird. A crow or a raven. When Sylvia tried to get a better look, it vanished, too.

"Does everyone look like they have auras to you?" she asked Emily.

Emily met her gaze over the top of the menu. "You're forgetting yourself. I'm the flaky one. You're the practical one. If anyone's going to see auras, it's going to be me."

"Do you?"

Her friend turned and looked. "No. Do you?"

"I think so."

Emily put down her menu, her eyes narrowed.

"Did you start celebrating early?"

"No!"

"But you're seeing auras. Uh huh. What's mine like?"

"You don't have one."

Emily pouted. "Who does?"

"That bartender has a green one that reminds me of a dragon, and the hostess has one that looks like snakes."

"Snakes?"

Sylvia nodded. "Black ones. And the one waitress has a black bird."

"Yuck." Emily shivered then looked again. This time, she straightened with interest. "How about *him*?"

Sylvia followed her friend's gaze and then she stared. A guy had appeared from somewhere and he was standing by the bar. He had dark hair and he was looking straight at her. No, he was staring. He was tall and lithe, really good looking, and apparently fascinated by her. When their gazes met, he didn't look away, and there was a hunger in his expression that made Sylvia shiver.

She blushed and looked back at her menu.

Was he an employee or a patron? Sylvia didn't know. He seemed to be lit by red neon from behind, like she wasn't supposed to miss him.

"Suddenly, it's a bit warm in here," Emily teased, then leaned across the table to whisper. "What's his aura like?"

Sylvia didn't have to look again. "Pulsing red."

"Like a volcano?"

"Like sex on demand, on red satin sheets, all weekend long." Sylvia could see the bedroom, the red and black wallpaper, the four-poster bed painted glossy black, the millions of candles—and the inescapable sense that the bed was an altar for worshipping pleasure. She swallowed, easily imagining his hand sliding over her skin in a smooth caress, that little smile—a lot like the one he was smiling now—then his possessive kiss...

"Happy birthday to you," Emily whispered gleefully. "You're getting wild already and I take full responsibility."

"I'm not getting wild..."

"Good evening, ladies," that very man said from beside their table. Sylvia jumped and his eyes glinted. He was even more gorgeous up close. His voice was deep and rich, and he spoke in a leisurely way, as if he had all the time in the world, as if he was savoring the feel of every syllable on his lips. His eyes were a strikingly vivid blue and his gaze was so piercing that she felt like hiding. He smiled a little more. "Anything to drink tonight?"

Sylvia was about to decline, thinking of their walk back to civilization, but Emily spoke up.

"Of course," she said with her usual cheerfulness. "It's my friend's birthday and we're out to celebrate."

"Happy birthday," he murmured, like a lover whispering sweet nothings in the night.

It was suddenly very hot in the restaurant.

"Thanks," Sylvia said, feeling a bit breathless. Either she'd been alone too long or this guy exuded sexual magnetism. She stole a peek and decided it was him.

"I read online about your pulled pork specialty and decided it would be exactly right for the occasion," Emily said.

"It's very popular," he agreed and Sylvia stole another glance. He was watching her. There was something intimate about his expression, as if they'd met before—no, as if they'd been lovers—but she knew she didn't know him.

His pulsing red aura, which made her think of sex and passion, pleasure and desire, didn't help.

"What's your meanest cocktail?" Emily asked.

"I thought you wanted a beer," Sylvia protested. If they started with mixed drinks, she really might do something she'd regret.

"I turned the page and changed my mind. All these pretty pictures." Emily smiled at the waiter. "Something really showy. Something we've never had before."

"Name Your Poison," he said smoothly.

"I just did," Emily complained.

"That's the name of the drink," Sylvia said, earning a quick glance from the waiter, and Emily laughed when she understood.

"We want two of those, and make them doubles."

"Emily! I have to work tomorrow."

"Tell me that anyone in the basement archives of

the library will notice if you're hung over."

"You're a librarian, then," the waiter with the dark chocolate voice asked. He actually seemed to be interested.

"Yes."

"She works at the—" Emily started to say, but Sylvia kicked her under the table. She was always providing too much information. "Too hard," Emily continued, trying to recover. "Working all the time, that's my studious friend. She misses out on real life."

Sylvia only shook her head, well accustomed to her friend's teasing. "You make up for me."

"And how!" Emily pointed at the waiter. "Five kids, two husbands—"

"At the same time?"

"Sadly, no," Emily replied quickly, then grinned. "Twice around the world, once on a boat, and now shacked up with my gingerbear in Podunk Junction."

"Content."

"Mostly." Emily smiled at him. "And you?"

"Old enough to be weary of the world and its tribulations," he acknowledged, his glance slanting to Sylvia. "But not of its pleasures."

Their gazes held for a simmering moment, one long enough for Sylvia's mouth to go dry.

"I'm starving," Emily said. "We'll have this combo platter with two kinds of fries and okra. We're officially living dangerously tonight."

"A salad," Sylvia said, but Emily waved off the

suggestion.

"There's always tomorrow for salad. Bring on the carbs and the meat, and we'll love it now, even if we regret it tomorrow morning."

"Savor the moment," their waiter said.

"Get it while you can," Emily agreed.

Sylvia shook her head, knowing that she'd never change Emily's mind. Portion control was the only thing that would save her.

"I'll just get those drinks," he said, managing to fill even those banal words with sensual promise. He sauntered back to the bar and Sylvia couldn't help herself—she checked out his butt.

"If you want to indulge in a private birthday celebration, I can go to a hotel," Emily whispered, as ready to facilitate as ever.

"You can't! It's too expensive."

"Then you can go to a hotel and I'll feed your cat before I catch the train in the morning. Promise."

"I don't have a cat."

"All the better. Less work for me."

"I'm not taking him home."

"Then go to his place."

"I'm not doing that either!"

"You should."

"Because it worked out so well last time."

"Oh, the jerk is gone." Emily never called Sylvia's ex by name. She'd hated Nolan that much. "They're not all losers like that big loser. And the only way you'll find a keeper is by getting into the pool again." She was already mixing metaphors and hadn't even had a drink yet.

"I need a little time."

"You need a couple of orgasms. Big screaming ones that make you bang your fists on the wall and wake up the neighbors. Have two and call me in the morning."

Of course, the waiter came back in time to hear Emily's advice. Sylvia could see that he was biting back a smile but she didn't meet his gaze. She did not want to have a conversation with this man about orgasms, hers or anyone else's.

Never mind two of them.

She could see that bedroom even more clearly, though. It was almost like a spell. It seemed that when he was close to her, each breath she took made the vision stronger, until she felt she could reach out and feel the velvet flocking on the wallpaper—or run one hand over his shoulder.

She closed her eyes and indulged in the vision. His lips were curved in that dangerous smile as he shut the door, sealing them into the chamber of pleasure. His eyes were filled with secrets, like deep wells she could jump into and never be found again. He crossed the room toward her, unfastening his shirt, gradually revealing his chest and her mouth went dry...

Sylvia picked up the drink, as much for something to do with her hands as anything else. It was green with fruit hanging on the side of the glass and there was something darker swirling in the bottom of the glass. She supposed it was intended to look like a poisonous potion. The fruit was on a miniature plastic dagger. She took a sip and felt as if she'd tasted liquid fire. That one small mouthful blazed a path to her stomach then combusted, leaving her seeing stars and feeling like her skin was on fire. She was sure she broke a sweat and that her knees were wobbly.

"This is good," Emily said, nodding approval after sipping her drink. "It tastes like lemonade, but with a bit of a kick."

"It tastes like nitro-glycerine," Sylvia said, pushing it aside.

"I wouldn't know," Emily said with a grin. "I've never tried that."

"Could I have a glass of wine, please?" she asked the waiter.

"Of course." He didn't ask her what kind, which was a bit odd, but before Sylvia could speak up, he slid something onto the table in front of her. "A little something from the management to commemorate your special day," he said in that sultry voice, the one that made all her good bits shiver. His hand lingered on it for a moment.

It was a book. A hardcover notebook.

She glanced up and his smile broadened. "Perhaps the perfect gift for a librarian," he added, inviting her to agree.

"Absolutely," Emily said. "Sylvia's the last person on the planet who loves paper books. I like my ebooks. I can take a whole library anywhere with me..."

"But there is a tactile pleasure to be savored with a physical book," their waiter said, his gaze never leaving Sylvia's. She wasn't even sure he blinked and she sure didn't want to look away.

She forced herself to look at the book. It had leather binding and could have been an antique. She picked it up and sniffed it.

He was visibly startled, but tried to hide it. "Nothing like the smell of a book."

"Nothing," she agreed, and smiled at him. Their gazes held for another intoxicating moment, Sylvia feeling as if her entire body was coming to life after a long sleep, then he nodded abruptly and returned to the bar.

"What are you doing?" Emily whispered with impatience. "It's just a plain old notebook, like the kind you get in an office supply store. At best, it smells like dust. Really, I think you must have started without me. He's going to think you're nuts, sniffing cheap notebooks."

When Sylvia looked again, it was just a plain notebook.

She frowned and picked it up, studying it more closely.

"A book," Emily said, rolling her eyes. "Why would they give something like that to someone on their birthday? That's just strange. There should have been cake. Whipped cream. A candle. Something decadent. Not a stupid notebook."

Sylvia didn't agree. She'd much rather have a

book than a dessert.

What was strange was that the book changed as she turned it in her hands. One moment, it was a plain notebook, just as Emily said. The next, it caught the light differently and appeared to be an antique. Then the binding was leather and the interior pages had ragged edges. Sylvia thought they were vellum, although in the dim light of the restaurant, it was hard to be sure. She opened it and was struck by the fact that it was filled with illustrations. She couldn't read the text. It might have been handwritten and it flowed around the illustrations in a very odd way. Maybe it wasn't even in English. She'd have to take a closer look in better light to be sure. The binding felt warm, and that couldn't be from his hand. Maybe it had been in a warm place, like on top of a radiator, because it felt hot beneath her hand.

She closed it and letters shimmered on the outside cover, like they were both there and not there.

Maeve's Book of Beasts. She shook her head because that made no sense to her.

Sylvia blinked and it was a notebook, filled with blank lined pages with no title on the cover. No matter how much she blinked and turned it, it stayed that way.

She was officially losing her mind.

Emily was halfway through her drink. "I thought you were Miss Manners," she chided, slurring her words a bit. "You didn't even thank him, even for a stupid book."

"You're right. I will when he comes back."

But he didn't come back. It was one of the waitresses who brought their food along with Sylvia's wine and took Emily's order for a second drink. She didn't like Sylvia's either, which meant they were different.

"What happened to our waiter?" Emily asked.

"What waiter?"

"The guy who took our drink order," Sylvia said.

The woman dropped her gaze. "There are no waiters here." Sylvia was trying not to stare at the ghostly black bird that seemed to hover behind her. It was both there and not there, because Sylvia could see the ceiling through it. But it was looking straight back at her, as if outraged that she was looking. Sylvia blinked and it disappeared. "The only guy who works here is Murray, the owner." The waitress indicated the burly older man who could have run a motorcycle gang on the side.

Emily and Sylvia exchanged glances. "But there was a guy," Emily insisted. "He brought us our drinks and took our order."

The waitress shook her head. "I took your order," she said, then pointed to the drink. "You've got to be careful with those."

"But he was here," Sylvia protested.

The waitress gestured to the bar, which was starting to get busier, inviting her to point him out. "Where?"

Sylvia knew even before she looked that she

wouldn't spot him. Her gaze fell on the book and she wondered just what it was—and why he'd given it to her.

It looked as if she'd have to figure that out herself.

"What's her aura like?" Emily whispered when the waitress walked away.

"She doesn't have one," Sylvia said, choosing to ignore the black bird. It was gone anyway.

Emily nodded with satisfaction. "See? You just needed a good meal. That's what you get for living on carrot sticks and cranberry juice. These fries are really good. Eat up, birthday girl!"

This was what happened when Sebastian trusted anyone else.

No, this was what happened when he allied with someone who failed to respect the power of magick. He knew better than to have anything to do with grimoires or other volumes of sorcery, and he certainly knew better than to mess with the dark queen, but Micah had found Sebastian's only point of weakness.

The key.

He would do anything for the key. He'd agreed to join the coven, he'd agreed to collect the book and later to deliver the book. He'd agreed to follow Micah's plan even though he didn't like it one bit, and now his part was done.

But Sebastian was snared. He couldn't even go

and collect his prize, the key, not now that he'd seen what he'd seen and heard what he'd heard.

Fucking magick.

He waited in a shadowed alley opposite Bones, oblivious to the damp wind coming off the river. He was so motionless and so dark that the few passersby thought him a shadow himself. The moon was one night from being new and he could see only the barest sliver of silver. The stars could be faintly discerned high overhead, and the sound of traffic dropped to a distant hum. He heard the sirens of the emergency vehicles, the patter of the first raindrops, the lapping of the river against the dock as the tide rose, the honking of distant horns.

He waited and he seethed.

He should just leave and let Micah's plan fall out badly. It wasn't his responsibility. It hadn't been his idea.

She hadn't been his suggestion.

And that was the problem. Sylvia was the problem. She wasn't oblivious to the true nature of the book, as Micah had said she would be. She could see what it was, Sebastian was certain of it, and that meant her custody of it was dangerous—to her. He wasn't fond of mortals, he was less fond of Others, and he was least fond of his own kind, but Sebastian hated when things were wrong.

He wouldn't call himself principled. He just liked to be right. He had argued against this plan, he had been told that he was wrong as well as reminded that he had agreed to bow to the collective will—

but he was *right*.

Sylvia knew.

She saw the truth of the book.

That would be the death of her.

And given the measure of kindness in the dark queen's black heart, it wouldn't be an easy demise.

Sebastian didn't want to feel responsible but that didn't change the fact that he did.

He should have walked away and gone to retrieve his key. Instead, he stood and waited, hoping for a sign that he was wrong.

He doubted there would be one.

The thirst came upon him with predictable timing and ferocity. It grew in intensity with every passing second. It made him twitch and burn. It made him think inappropriate thoughts about Sylvia—a librarian! So delicious that he'd been tempted to bend down and just take a nibble. That long sleek neck, such fair skin, such thick hair—was it brown or auburn? He hadn't been sure—and her inviting scent. Heat and blood and perfume and woman. He growled in the dark and clenched his fists. Her secrets had almost been begging to be unfurled—by him and no one else. Sebastian wanted as he seldom wanted, and he knew it wasn't just the thirst.

There was something about Sylvia.

Something dangerous, even to him.

This was what happened when those who didn't respect magick under-estimated its chaotic power. Sebastian hated grimoires and magickal tomes of all kinds, but he respected them.

Micah didn't.

For all Sebastian knew, the book itself had created this trouble, and he resented its manipulation thoroughly.

He didn't like this bar. He didn't like his neighbor, Melusine, and he didn't like Murray, the dwarf who ran the bar. He didn't like being surrounded by so many Others at Bones or anywhere else, and he certainly didn't want to talk to any of them about their powers, abilities or fears. He hated being in Micah's coven.

In fact, having to surrender his solitude in order to fight the dark queen only made Sebastian despise her even more. The sooner this was resolved, the better.

He only wanted to be alone, and that hadn't changed since 1450. He lived for one appetite alone and had for a long time. It was odd to feel an old hunger stirring again.

And inconvenient.

Sylvia.

It was a seductive name. Musical. Feminine. It was ridiculous, but if she'd been named Maggie or Kate, he would have been more immune to her allure. Sebastian knew better than to be seduced, although he was tempted—and that reaction intrigued him more than was healthy.

Sylvia was attractive, but not so conscious of her charms that she flaunted them. In fact, she seemed to have a protective armor against the world. If she'd trusted once and been betrayed, all the better. Her wariness would make it harder for Maeve or anyone else to trick her.

Mortal women were more trouble than they were worth, he reminded himself, and he would never willingly turn anyone. He shuddered at the prospect of being bound to another individual forever. Nothing could be worse.

Nothing except maybe feeling himself being drawn into an emotional web again.

Sylvia.

Only ignorance of what she'd been given would save her. The best way to hide a secret from Maeve was to be ignorant of it. The dark queen could read thoughts, no matter how deeply they were buried. No one could hide a secret from her.

Which meant the book had to be entrusted to someone unlikely and unexpected, someone who had no clue what it was, someone whose situation meant that it could be easily retrieved. Micah had chosen the librarian, but Sebastian couldn't dismiss his sense that Sylvia had glimpsed the book's truth.

Had the book chosen to reveal itself to her?

What about that vision of a red and black room, a scene set for seduction? Where had that come from? And why? Sebastian didn't know where that bedroom was located. Was it hers? He found the black and red decor an unlikely choice for such a reserved woman. The sight of her, gaze clinging to his, taking the pins out of her hair, licking her lips, awaiting his touch, luminous and welcoming and aroused, turned his thoughts in a much more earthly direction.

Had they shared a glimpse of the future? If so, why? Sebastian knew he hadn't conjured the vision, and really, it had felt as if he had simply fallen into it.

He'd heard Sylvia explaining to her friend that she was seeing auras. The friend, like most mortals, was oblivious to ninety-nine per cent of what was happening around her and skeptical. It was definitely a problem if Sylvia could see the hidden truth of the Others.

He was inclined to think the book had prompted a change in Sylvia, given that she'd been surprised by the auras. He couldn't ignore his sense that the book was changing the rules, maybe just as the dark queen had commanded.

This was the trouble with books stolen from powerful sorcerers. It was impossible to know what they could do. He hadn't liked having this one in his possession for even a day.

He was tempted to reclaim the book, but he'd promised to do as instructed. He should walk away, go hunt, satisfy the thirst.

But Sebastian couldn't.

He should have remained alone.

CHAPTER TWO

ury shot through Sebastian when he smelled company.

He looked down to find that a silver wolf had appeared and now crouched at his feet. It wasn't just a stray dog. He could smell otherwise. Sebastian snarled at the werewolf and that creature bared his teeth, as if laughing at Sebastian. The wolf's eyes were different colors, one silver and one blue, and there was something chilling about his stare.

Another predator.

One more of the Others.

The wolf trotted across the road and sat outside the restaurant, clearly waiting for Sylvia. This was not good.

Was this werewolf allied with the Others? Or was it on a quest of its own? The wolf shifters were loyal to each other but not necessarily to anyone else. Sebastian knew they were listed in the book, and wondered if he'd run his fingertip over this one's name.

It had chilled him to see his own there.

Sebastian's temper flared as the door opened. He couldn't meet Sylvia outside the restaurant without raising her suspicions that he was a stalker or some other individual to be feared. He had to protect her, even from himself, and that didn't improve his mood.

He watched, powerless, as the women emerged onto the street.

The one in purple, predictably, stopped to pat what she thought was a dog. The werewolf stood and wagged his tail at her, inviting her to underestimate his lethal power.

She did. She patted him on the head and talked to him in baby talk.

Sylvia pulled her friend forcibly away, showing better sense. "It could have fleas, Emily," she said with disgust. "Or bite you."

"He wouldn't bite. He's a good doggie-woggie."

"Take a look at him! He looks more like a wolf. And those teeth. Let's get out of here already." Sylvia tugged her friend up the street, moving at a brisk pace even as the friend looked back.

The wolf sat watching them, tail swishing on the sidewalk.

When they were out of sight, he turned to Sebastian, as if to issue a challenge.

Sebastian wondered if all the old injunctions about drinking from other kinds were really deserved. He thought it might be worth an experiment. He could think of one candidate he'd be glad to sacrifice to the search for knowledge. The thirst raged and he took a step forward, knowing he looked fearsome when the thirst was this strong.

The werewolf barked, then cantered after the women. His walk was uneven, as if he favored one leg, but that didn't slow him down.

Sebastian swore and leaped for a fire escape. He climbed to the roof of the building with lightning speed and set off after the women, leaping from roof to roof. It was easy to spot them, given how quiet the streets had become.

They had linked arms as they marched quickly toward the busier thoroughfare several blocks away. The werewolf left the alley, trotting to intersect the women's path in a more busy area. Sebastian flitted from shadow to shadow behind the women, watching over them protectively, wondering how long the book would be safe in Sylvia's care.

Thirsting for blood all the while.

What would Micah do if Sebastian reclaimed the book?

His key would be sacrificed, if not more.

"He's following us!" the friend cried with delight when she spun to find the werewolf behind them.

Sylvia eyed the dog with justified suspicion and hailed a cab. She shoved her friend into it and the werewolf was left behind for the moment. Sebastian had little time to feel triumphant. The wolf disappeared into an alley. Sebastian lost track of him and didn't care, for the moment. He ran across rooftops, following Sylvia's scent. It was exhilarating to run and not that hard to keep up to the taxi in the evening press of traffic. They headed toward Gramercy Park. When the cab slowed in front of a townhouse converted to apartments, Sebastian descended to an adjacent alley to watch.

Their destination was a gracious house with broad stairs rising from the sidewalk and a double-doored entry. There was a small patio with a gate, reached by half a dozen steps that descended from the sidewalk. Once, this level would have been the servant's quarters, with the kitchen in the back. The first floor was a few steps above the street, and he could see that there were three more above it. The top one was smallest, with a patio across the front.

To Sebastian's dismay, a man stood at the top of the steps to the townhouse, carrying a large box. He had silver hair, cut short in a military style, and wore jeans and boots with a leather jacket. When he glanced up, clearly sensing Sebastian's presence, Sebastian saw that his eyes were different colors.

One was silver and one was blue.

The smell of him proved Sebastian's suspicions. He wasn't a man. He was a werewolf and worse, the same werewolf that had been outside the bar. Sebastian wanted to snarl—or better yet, rip out the werewolf's throat and solve the problem.

But if he revealed himself to intervene, Sylvia

would wonder how he'd found her home, how he'd arrived there before her, and undoubtedly distrust him once she witnessed what he could do. His chance of retrieving the book easily from her would drop to nil and his ability to protect her while she possessed it would be seriously compromised. She might become curious about the book, and closer inspection could only put her in more peril.

He hadn't liked Micah's plan in the first place, and he liked it less with every passing moment.

That's what he got for joining a team.

The werewolf gave a hard look at the shadow that was Sebastian, like a warning, then glanced toward the cab at the curb. He tipped the box so he was holding most of its weight in one hand, and flicked through keys with the other.

No. The shifter couldn't be *living* in Sylvia's building.

Sebastian wanted to rage. His hatred of werewolves hit new heights, but there was nothing he could do for the moment.

But watch, wait, and burn with the thirst.

No, not even that. Bella touched his sleeve, having approached with her usual silence. "You need to feed," she said.

"I can wait..."

"Micah says you might draw attention to her if you don't leave her alone."

Sebastian inhaled sharply, more than ready to give Bella a terse message to take back to Micah. He wasn't some obedient lap dog, to be commanded at every moment, even if he had reluctantly joined the team.

But his key.

Bella leaned closer, dropped her voice and whispered. "You promised," she reminded him, her eyes glittering with the fire of the thirst.

Sebastian didn't appreciate the reminder. If nothing else, he knew he would think more clearly after he fed.

"I found some perfect candidates," she said, knowing that he preferred to hunt alone. Sebastian slanted a glance at her, wondering why she wanted to share. They were both loners, and he liked that about Bella. "It'll be easy. Just like last time."

"You found them already?"

"Bad enough now and they'll be worse when they come out of that bar. One for you and one for me. You'll be back in no time."

Sebastian was very tempted. One benefit of hunting with Bella is that she always had a plan.

And it usually adhered to Micah's rules. He wasn't so inclined to behave in Micah's terms, but felt their alliance was on thin ice. Defiance over victims wouldn't help his cause—or get his key back.

"I have to be sure she gets home," he said, drawing a line in the proverbial sand. Bella rolled her eyes but ceded the point. She seethed with restless energy and it was contagious, so that even Sebastian tapped his toe with impatience for Sylvia to lock her own door behind herself.

"Werewolves," Bella hissed, finally catching a whiff. She did have a tendency to ignore the obvious when she was thirsty.

"Just one so far."

"They're like cockroaches," Bella scoffed. "There's never just one."

"Exactly," Sebastian agreed and folded his arms across his chest to wait.

There was a guy on the porch of the townhouse where Sylvia lived, juggling a moving box as he sorted through his keys. He was trim but muscular, with short silver hair. Something about his appearance made Sylvia think he might be in the service. He was dressed simply but neatly in a leather jacket and jeans. He seemed to be favoring one leg a little bit.

Maybe he wasn't in the service anymore.

She was startled when she spotted the ghost of a silver wolf above and behind him, just like the auras of the people at the bar. She hadn't seen another since leaving there.

Weird how the ghost looked like the dog that had befriended Emily.

Sylvia shivered.

"Silver fox alert," Emily murmured as Sylvia was paying the fare, and she wondered if her friend saw the aura, too. Before she could ask, Emily was out of the cab and talking to the guy. "Moving in?" she asked and he spared her a wary glance.

Emily wasn't shy, that was for sure.

"Just trying to sort out these keys," he said with a nod. His voice was low and he spoke calmly and slowly. "I thought this was for the front door."

"No, it's that one," Emily said, pointing to another key on his ring.

"How do you know?"

"I'm staying here."

He surveyed her, his gaze flicking to Sylvia, then fitted the key into the lock, putting his booted foot in the door. "So you say. You'll need to come in with your own key," he said, showing a lot better sense than Emily in Sylvia's view.

"I don't have one. Sylvia lives here. I'm just visiting."

His brows rose at this wealth of information and his gaze landed on Sylvia again. She could feel the intensity of his attention from ten feet away and smiled. "Sorry about my friend. She's from a small town."

"You should be more careful about sharing personal details," he told Emily sternly. He nodded at Sylvia. "If you really have keys, I'll see you inside." Then he went inside and let the door shut behind himself.

"Not very friendly," Emily huffed.

"But sensible," Sylvia said. "I like that."

"Really?"

"I don't want to live in a building where the other tenants just let anybody in. That compromises security. Eithne would have my head if I encouraged that kind of thing."

"Eithne," Emily muttered. "Does she even exist?"

"Of course!"

"When did you see her last?"

"She lives right down there, on the garden floor."

"When did you see her last?" Emily repeated.

Sylvia thought about it. "Two weeks ago. She gave me a check to pay the property taxes."

"Did she tell you about him?"

"No. I thought the whole building was let." Sylvia put her key into the lock and opened the door. The overhead light was on in the downstairs foyer and the door to 2F, the unit at the front of the main floor was open. The guy they'd just met was standing there, the box on the floor blocking the doorway. It was the smallest apartment in the house, which said something in that they were all studio apartments except for Sylvia's. The stairway was flush against the left wall and the door to 2B was at the end of the hall beside the stairway. It was closed, though Sylvia guessed that Rachel might be watching through the peephole.

"What happened to Carlos?" Sylvia asked.

The guy shrugged. "Was that who lived here before?"

"Until this morning."

"I don't know." This time, he smiled and offered his hand. Sylvia blinked at the change in his appearance. "Caleb Davison," he said. His grip was firm and Sylvia had an impression that he was reliable. "Just moving in."

"So I see. Sylvia Fontaine. I'm on the top floor."

"Nice to meet you. I hope my dog doesn't bother you. He doesn't usually bark but you never know in a new place."

"You have a dog?!" Emily asked, starting toward his apartment with purpose.

Caleb glanced over his shoulder. "He finally crashed after being on patrol all day. Don't wake him up, please." His smile was affectionate and made him look a lot less stern. "And when you see him, don't be afraid. He's big but friendly, unless there's a good reason not to be."

"I didn't know Eithne allowed dogs," Emily said.

Caleb shrugged. "She didn't say. Maybe she made an exception for me. Loki and I worked together in the K-9 unit when I was a cop. He really took a liking to her earlier."

Sylvia blinked. Her aunt had found a new tenant within hours of Carlos moving out? That had to be a record. Usually, she asked Sylvia to solve it, after a unit had been empty for a week.

"You're not a cop any more?" Emily asked.

Caleb tapped his left leg. "Taking a slug changes everything. Early retirement isn't so bad, plus I have a new job as a security guard."

"That sounds like a good way to use your skills," Sylvia said, heading for the stairs.

He laughed a little, and it was a good rich sound. "Sort of. It's at a circus, which is kind of different.

Wait." He ducked into his apartment and returned with a flyer. He did have a limp, but Sylvia pretended she hadn't noticed. He gave the flyer to her. "If you ever want to go, let me know. I can get you a discount on admission."

"How long is it here?"

He shrugged. "They said months. We'll see. It's pretty busy, especially on Fridays."

Circus of Wonders. She'd never heard of it.

"A circus," Emily whispered. "We could go tomorrow."

"You're going back to Podunk tomorrow," Sylvia reminded her.

Emily winced. "I can't change my ticket, either. It was too good of a deal. I'll have to come back another time."

"In less than a year," Sylvia teased and they laughed together. She said goodnight to Caleb and led Emily upstairs, well aware that he was watching them go. She heard his door close and lock, then the growl of a large dog. "I kind of like the idea of having an ex-cop in the building," she said to Emily as they climbed the stairs. "And his dog."

There were three flights of stairs to Sylvia's apartment, with two studio rentals on each floor. It was a longer climb than might have been expected, because the house had twelve-foot ceilings. Sylvia loved it, though, as well as the sweeping wooden bannister that coiled all the way up to the top floor. There was an oval skylight over the staircase on the roof, and she liked how the light flooded through the townhouse.

She often thought of how beautiful it must have been as a single family home. The floors were hardwood and there was a fireplace in each unit—which meant there were two fireplaces in her apartment, the only one that took up an entire floor. With terraces front and back and sloped roofs, though, it wasn't exactly enormous.

"Especially in the unit beside the front door," Emily agreed, huffing a little.

"Eithne must have been thinking the same thing."

"You can't be too safe in this city."

"Right. That's why you tell everyone your business, even before they ask." Sylvia softened her words with a smile and unlocked the door to her apartment.

Emily dropped on the couch and kicked off her shoes. "I know. I'm just a country bumpkin. I forget to *not* be friendly." She laid down and closed her eyes. "That drink was killer. I could fall asleep right now."

"And you'll have a headache tomorrow, I bet."

The main room of Sylvia's apartment had a kitchenette along one wall and a seating area, littered with books. The terrace ran the width of the house and faced roughly north east, which made it a cool refuge in the summer. The mechanicals in the house rose in a column beside the staircase, so all units had their bathrooms there, and Sylvia had the best closet. Her bedroom faced the front of the house, with another terrace, although this one was filled with planters. That southern exposure was great for her containers.

Sylvia got her friend a big glass of water and a pair of aspirin. By the time she turned around, though, Emily was asleep on the couch with her mouth open. As Sylvia smiled, Emily started to snore.

"Just like college," Sylvia murmured and lifted Emily's legs onto the couch. She left the water and aspirin on the coffee table, in case Emily woke up, then pulled a blanket over her. She turned down the lights, then felt a prickle on the back of her neck. Sylvia turned quickly, halfway thinking there had been motion on the terrace.

But there was nothing there.

What was wrong with her tonight? She made a cup of decaf tea to settle her nerves and pulled the book out of her purse. It looked like a notebook again, but then if she turned her head a little sideways and squinted at it, it became an ancient tome once more.

Sylvia pulled up a stool and opened the book on the kitchen counter. She saw plain lined pages first, but then the same trick of tilting her head revealed the vellum pages with ragged edges. They looked to be covered with magical inscriptions, or words in a language she couldn't read, and illustrations that seemed very old. There was new writing in it, too, in dark red ink. They looked like dates.

Like here. There was a section with drawings of

mermaids. Mermaids on rocks, combing their hair. Mermaids kissing sailors, their hair flowing around them both. Mermaids in the sea, their tails glittering and glistening. Then a red X and what looked like a date five years before.

What did it mean?

Here was a unicorn in a field of flowers, then another galloping through the forest with what had to be a maiden riding it bareback. Here was a third unicorn, its head in the lap of a maiden who gazed down at it with adoration. She seemed to have woven it a harness of daisies. Again, a red X, and a date—in 1853.

Was it an inventory?

But how could fantastical beasts be associated with calendar dates?

Sylvia's sense that she was being watched got stronger and she shuddered. She checked the door and the windows, pulled the drapes and went to bed, telling herself that it was exhaustion at work.

But was it?

Bella led Sebastian back toward the meatpacking district where Bones was located. She turned down a quiet side street, one with a few alleys and not many windows. The windows that did face the street were high, and dark. There were clouds slipping across that sliver of moon and the street was devoid of traffic.

A pair of young men stumbled onto the street

from the busier avenue ahead. "I tell you, the car is parked down here," one said, his words slurred.

"You don't know where you left the car, you loser," the other said, his drunken voice filled with laughter. "You never know where you leave the car."

"At least I have a car."

"At least I have money for beer, because I don't have a car." They laughed much harder at this than Sebastian thought it deserved, then continued to stagger down the street.

"Look, there it is."

"That's blue, dude. Your car is *green*."

"It's blue."

"The last one was blue. Your new car is green."

"Damn. You mean I lost a new car? And I don't even remember it?" Again they laughed, but Bella touched Sebastian's arm.

Just like last time. He nodded understanding and stayed in the shadows.

Bella stepped out of the alley and walked quickly down the street toward the two young men. Sebastian smiled at her skill in pretending to be much younger than she was. He'd known her almost five hundred years, but anyone would guess that she was a mortal girl of maybe eighteen. She was blonde and petite, her hair flowing long down her back, her features delicate and pretty. On this night, she was dressed in pink and black, feminine and girlish. She was looking at something in her hand that could have been a cell phone and carrying a tote bag with a Hello Kitty logo, apparently oblivious to her surroundings.

How many had underestimated her strength over those centuries? How many had failed to see her truth?

Sebastian knew there would be two more very soon.

The two young men straightened when they spotted her and stepped toward her as one, predators on the hunt. Bella continued to march straight toward them, apparently unaware of their attention. Sebastian could smell their lust, how it drove the haze of alcohol away, as well as their complete lack of compunction in taking whatever they wanted, no matter who paid the price.

Bella had chosen well, as ever. Micah would have no quibbles with this pair leaving the world of the living.

"Hey, there," one of them said when she was just ten feet in front of them.

Bella jumped, apparently startled, and dropped her phone. "Oh!" she said, with maidenly dismay.

The two moved closer, flanking her. One picked up her phone. "Are you lost?" the other asked.

"I'm just, I'm just trying to get home," Bella said, her voice high with fear.

"Bet you'd like this back," said the one with the phone.

"It's my phone! Yes, please."

"How badly do you want it back?" asked the other.

Bella made an incoherent sound of dismay.

"Bad enough to trade a kiss for it?" asked the one with the phone. They closed around her, one on each side, and she looked between them in fear. One laughed. The other reached for her. Bella took a step back to an alley that was so close Sebastian knew she'd planned to encounter them right beside it.

"Just a quick one. And not where anyone can see," she said, her manner suddenly coy. She giggled, flicking glances between them, then beckoned to the one with the phone. The two men exchanged triumphant glances and the one without the phone gave his buddy a thumb's up. Bella laughed, her manner flirtatious, and disappeared into the alley. Her prey followed her willingly.

The other one strolled back and forth on the sidewalk, grinning at his friend's score.

Sebastian strode down the street with purpose, like a respectable man returning home. He stared at the young man as if offended by his presence, looking him up and down. "Are you loitering?" he demanded with indignation.

"Just waiting for my friend."

"I don't see any friend," Sebastian said. "I suggest you move along, before I'm obliged to call the police..."

The man raised a hand, as if he'd negotiate, and Bella gave a little gasp of terror in that moment.

Sebastian spun to glare into the alley. "What's that? What's going on in there? That was a woman!

What is your *friend* doing to her?" He charged into the alley, rushing to the defense of the woman in jeopardy, knowing the friend would be right behind him.

He was.

Sebastian stepped aside, letting him see Bella feasting on his friend. She crouched above her victim beside a Dumpster, her skin fair in contrast to the blood flowing from the wound in his neck. She looked feral and dangerous as she drained him, and her victim's expression was one of shock.

The fly of his jeans was open, showing the true measure of his character and intentions. Blood ran from the wound there, staining the denim and the ground.

"What the..." the friend whispered, then pivoted to run. He didn't even manage to take a step before Sebastian seized him from behind, hurled him to the ground, then ripped open his throat. The last sound he made was a moan after the blood gurgled forth—lovely, luscious, rich red blood. Sebastian drank, feeling the power surge through him, feeling the thirst sated and his energy rebuild. He devoured his victim's essence quickly, sucking him all the way dry.

The thirst had been strong.

In Sebastian's experience, there were leisurely feasts and quick snacks. Although he had never turned anyone, there had been a few times when he had considered it. There were vampires who had turned victims with poor technique, but not

Sebastian. Now he was old and practiced and efficient.

He cast away the carcass of his victim, feeling sated and warm. Triumphant. Bella threw aside hers with disgust, and Sebastian could see that his corpse was dry as well. She indicated the Dumpster and they easily lifted the two bodies into it. There was already a collection of trash there. Bella took the inevitable bottle of lighter fluid from her Hello Kitty bag and emptied it over the corpses before turning to Sebastian.

"Are you doing the honors this time?" she asked, and he nodded.

Micah did not like them to leave any obvious signs of their feeding. Questions from mortals complicated matters unnecessarily—and there were always questions when corpses were found devoid of blood with punctures at the neck.

"Remember you have to report," Bella reminded him. "He's waiting."

Sebastian nodded. He felt less agitated now that the thirst was satisfied, but still was disgruntled.

What if he could retrieve his key, and then take the book from Sylvia? He didn't want anything to do with that volume, but he also couldn't stand aside and watch Micah's plan fall into chaos.

Not if Sylvia's life was the price.

It was just because he was right, not because he cared or had a sense of responsibility, much less a moral code.

Bella turned her coat inside out, so that the black

side was out, and headed for the fire escape at the end of the alley. Sebastian watched her go, noting how quickly she seemed to disappear into her surroundings. They could pass easily amongst humans now that they'd fed, but there was no reason to be observed coming out of this alley.

He struck the match, cast it into the Dumpster and watched the flames catch before he strode after Bella.

He wanted his key.

Sylvia dreamed of the book.

At least, she thought she was dreaming.

The book was on her kitchen counter, just where she had left it. The apartment was filled with shadows, but a stray beam of moonlight came through the crack between the curtains on the window over the sink. The moonlight touched the book like a silver wand.

She saw the book shimmer, like it had been illuminated from within.

It fluttered, its pages making a tinkling sound.

It opened of its own accord, the pages fanning in the moonlight.

Sylvia wasn't in bed. She was in the doorway to the main room of her apartment, opposite the terrace and beside the bathroom. Emily was sleeping on her back on the couch, her breathing heavy. There was a feeling of electricity in the air again, as if lightning had hit somewhere close. Sylvia felt goosepimples rise as a chill swept over her flesh.

"You have my book," a woman whispered, her voice dark with anger. Sylvia scanned her apartment but she couldn't see anyone. "Thief!"

There was a haze over the book, like a cloud of silver fireflies.

Sylvia eased closer, her heart racing.

"Give back my book, Thief," the woman said. "Return it now."

The fireflies, if that was what they were, flowed upward like a flock of birds against a summer sky. A murmuration, that's what it was called, a mesmerizing wavy pattern of motion. Sylvia stared, unable to keep from doing so, and moved closer.

"Where are you, Thief?" the woman asked, as if anyone with any sense would confide in her. Her voice was oily and untrustworthy. Dangerous. "Show yourself, Thief."

Sylvia licked her lips and moved to the end of the counter. The little lights that looked like fireflies were small creatures. Hundreds of them, all silvery, all flying in the light of the moon. The book's pages with alive with golden writing that danced and seethed across the pages, script of molten gold or liquid fire.

"Where have you hidden my book, Thief?" the woman whispered, her voice a little bit louder. The fireflies moved with greater agitation, forming into a spiral.

Like a tornado.

It spun faster and faster, the pages of the book

lifting in its wind. Sylvia felt her hair blow and snap around her face. The pizza coupons from her mail box that she'd left on the counter blew suddenly to the floor. She heard a dog bark sharply as the pictures on the walls of her apartment began to rock in the wind from the fireflies.

"What makes you think you can deceive me?" the woman roared.

Sylvia reached out quickly, flicked the book shut and shoved it off the counter onto the floor. It landed with a thud in the darkness. The fireflies disappeared and the wind stopped. The moon must have moved behind a cloud because the finger of moonlight was gone and Sylvia shivered at the sudden chill in her apartment.

Emily slept on.

The dog barked again, then sniffed audibly at the bottom of the door to the hall before retreating.

"Loki!" a man said, chiding the dog from the stairway. The stairs creaked beneath the weight of his steps. "Come, Loki!"

It was Caleb and his dog.

He tapped once on Sylvia's door, softly, such a quiet tap that it wouldn't have awakened her if she was sleeping.

"Yes," Sylvia managed to say. She didn't open the door.

"Everything all right?" There was something reassuring about his concern, and his presence. She liked that the dog had heard the book's ruckus.

Sylvia looked at the book, which looked like a

cheap notebook on her kitchen floor. "Fine," she said, trying to sound cheerful. "Just a bad dream."

"Sorry about the dog," Caleb said.

"No, it's fine. Thanks for checking on us."

He mumbled something, maybe "It's what I do," and then Sylvia heard his footfalls on the stairs as he went back to his apartment.

Funny how no one else in the building had heard anything. Celeste, the widow in 4F, didn't miss much but she hadn't made a sound.

Maybe she was away.

Sylvia picked up the book, turning it over once, then looked around for somewhere to put it where no moonlight could touch it. The bottom of her purse seemed like the best choice. She wedged it in there and went back to bed.

She didn't think she'd go back to sleep easily but she was wrong.

CHAPTER THREE

he meeting convened as soon as the last human patron left Bones. Murray had barely locked the door when the Others began to arrive. Those who worked at the bar were already there, of course. The rest arrived through the doors hidden in the basement or flowed down from the access to the roof. As Mel had anticipated, it was an anxious crowd, ready for debate, and the bar was full of arguing Others within moments. Murray turned up the lights and Mel started to pull glasses of draft beer. Each one was taken as soon as she placed it on the counter and she hoped the kegs were full.

Mel also hoped the meeting was short. It was Sunday already and she could feel the weekly change beginning deep inside, like a portent of doom. By dawn, her involutary shift would be complete and it would last until the last bit of daylight faded. She wanted to be home with the door locked and a good book before that happened.

She couldn't help but notice that the vampires were absent.

Murray came to work beside her, his brow furrowed, and pulled glasses of beer as quickly as he could.

"Didn't you invite the vampires?" she asked him in an undertone and he shook his head.

"I thought we should discuss their part first."

"They shouldn't even have a part in this," said a wolf shifter as he claimed two glasses. "They aren't part of it."

"He had the book," Mel said. "That made him part of it."

"It didn't give them the right to decide," Kara, the Valkyrie waitress said as she put glasses of beer on a tray. She carried them to a table of djinn who started to make the beer disappear.

"Actually, it did," Murray observed. "Possession being nine tenths of the law and all that."

"We didn't have to go along with it," the wolf shifter argued. Mel couldn't remember his name. Truth be told, she had a hard time distinguishing between the werewolves, since they acted so similarly. This one wasn't Caleb, their leader, because his eyes were both blue. Caleb had heterochromia, which made him a little bit more distinctive.

He wasn't the only wolf shifter with eyes of different colors, though.

"How else would we know what they did with it?" Murray asked. "Letting them use Bones to hide the book was our best way of ensuring that we knew where it was."

"You could have just asked us," Micah said mildly. As was characteristic—and irritating—of vampires, he had slipped into the bar with the silence of a shadow. Mel shivered as the temperature dropped. Rosemary was with him, looking so cool and dispassionate that it was hard to believe it hadn't been long since Micah had turned her.

A ripple passed through the company and the vampires were given a lot of room.

There were only the two of them, at least so far.

"You wouldn't have told us," accused Kara. "Vampires never play for the team."

"We're not on the team," Micah said, his tone reasonable. "Yet. But with a welcome like this, we might not ever be."

"No loss there," said the wolf shifter to general agreement.

"And these are the ones left to defend mankind," Raymond murmured. "If I were alive, I would give serious consideration to taking my chances with Maeve."

Although Mel agreed with her ex in this particular matter, she didn't respond to him. While she was keenly aware of him in his ghostly form, most others—even Others—couldn't see and hear him. Talking to an invisible man wouldn't give her decision-making any credibility.

She could feel the delicate union of Others starting to fracture and knew they'd all be lost if they didn't stick together. Building consensus at this meeting was crucial.

She'd wondered before if the werewolves smelled Raymond and wondered again when the one at the bar tipped his head back and narrowed his eyes. His nostrils flared and he looked behind Mel intently, but he didn't seem to see Raymond.

She wasn't sure whether to be relieved or not.

"We have to stick together," she said to the Others who had gathered. "And we need to find more of Maeve's targets. We need to build this alliance, not destroy it. She has so many advantages, and we need every one we can get."

"Let her have the vampires," the wolf shifter said. "That should keep her quiet for a century or two."

"And then what?" Murray challenged. "And then she comes for the werewolves, or the djinns, or the Valkyries. She's immortal and most of us aren't." He nodded to Mel who dropped her gaze. She didn't really think it had been necessary for Murray to remind them of that. "The mermaids are gone, the unicorns, the elves. She's taken the centaurs and the elves. It's just a matter of time before she eliminates all of us. I say we eliminate her."

There wasn't rousing agreement to that

sentiment. Instead, the Others exchanged worried glances.

"But how?" asked a selkie. "She can slip between realms. She can retreat to Fae, and the portals to that realm are closed against all who aren't of her kind."

"She can read our most secret thoughts," agreed a djinn.

"Nothing can be hidden from her," the wolf shifter said grimly and drained his beer.

"Which was why we had to entrust the book to an ordinary mortal who had no idea what it was," Micah said. "Someone who can't even perceive what it is. That's the only way to keep it safe."

The Others exchanged glances. "But how do we find out what's in it?" asked the medusa who worked as hostess.

"We borrow it," Micah said softly. "And we do so without the custodian being aware of our presence or our interference. In this way, the book will remain safe the vast majority of the time."

"But?" the wolf shifter invited.

Micah shrugged. "There will be risks when we endeavor to look at it. The dark queen may be aware of our movements." He cleared his throat. "I suggest we accept volunteers."

"Easy for you to say, when you're immortal like her," the wolf shifter snarled.

"Even an immortal can be killed," Micah countered. "Is that not right, Kara?"

The Valkyrie took a deep breath and glared at

him. "Don't put me in your camp, vampire."

"But we have that common ground," he countered. "My kind are immortal, as are yours. Others here, with the exception of Mel and her curse, may be long-lived but are mortal."

"That doesn't mean she doesn't want us exterminated," Kara said.

"No, it does not," Micah agreed softly. "We're still beasts and brutes in her view, neither pure Fae nor human."

There was a ripple of discontent at that.

"If we work together, we can each contribute our strengths," Mel said. "We can cooperate to ensure each other's safety until she's destroyed."

There was a stirring at this notion, then a large bear shifter stepped forward. "How do we know she can be destroyed?"

"Everyone and everything can be destroyed," Murray said with conviction. He smiled. "We just have to work out the details."

This answer didn't give much satisfaction. "What we need are all the Others joined together," Mel said again.

"I don't see any dragons," said the wolf shifter.

"I'm getting there," Mel said. "They're not really social."

The bear shifter grunted at that. "We'll do it without them."

"I think they're important," Mel insisted but the bear shifter was unconvinced.

"How are we to know that the vampires can be

trusted?" the wolf shifter asked. "They haven't joined our alliance or sworn to fight with all of us. This could be a trick." He turned to Micah. "You could be on *her* side."

"And why would we do that?" Micah asked, his voice sharpening a little. "What possible temptation could there be in surrendering to her will?"

"She might give you perks for betraying us," the bear shifter said.

"She would place us in thrall," Micah whispered. "She would take our freedom. We would be enslaved, trapped in Fae and left to shrivel to nothing. Captivity would destroy us forever." He fixed the wolf shifter with a look. "Surely we have that in common."

The wolf shifter frowned. "You should swear an oath."

"In blood?" Micah asked, lifting a brow.

"Each and every one of you," the wolf shifter insisted. "We know it's not your inclination to work together."

"That might have been true once, but she has taken most of my kind," Micah admitted. Mel exchanged a surprised glance with Murray. Vampires were notoriously secretive and solitary but she hadn't known that. Murray's brows rose and she knew he hadn't known either. "All that is left is my coven, the Coven of Mercy."

"Coven of *mercy*?" the bear shifter spat.

"We agreed to take the ill and the wounded as our prey, or worst case, the wicked," Rosemary explained, her words clipped and precise. "In the realms of hunter and hunted, the weakest always become prey. We choose to help in culling the herd, rather than taking prime specimens who have a contribution to make to human society. It doesn't matter to us: we just need the blood to survive. Human illness doesn't affect us. But it makes a healthier codependency."

Micah took her hand. "And we work together, the thirteen of us. I believe that is what saved us, or has saved us so far."

"So, you would join our alliance," Mel said, relieved and surprised. She'd expected more of a fight from the vampires.

"And you can share the contents of the book with us," the wolf shifter insisted.

"You all know what's in it," Micah said with a shake of his head. "Every species she considers an abomination is listed, along with the names of every surviving member of that species."

"She strikes them off the list," the bear shifter said gruffly, seizing his beer and taking a gulp.

"Actually, I would have liked to have a look inside," Mel said, still annoyed that the vampires had whisked the book away.

"We don't need to learn more about the dark queen," Micah said sternly.

"We can use the list to find all of the Others," Mel said. "And bring them into our alliance."

Micah sighed. "In my experience, the most successful quests have small teams."

"So, you routinely take out dark Fae queens?" the bear shifter asked and there was laughter at the very idea.

Micah frowned. "I think it's dangerous to look inside."

The wolf shifter scoffed then pushed his glass across the bar, his manner impatient. Mel started to pour him another beer.

"But we don't know where she'll strike next," a djinn protested.

"Of course, we do," another man said, his voice so low and rich that he had to be a vampire. He stepped out of the shadows behind Micah, and she recognized the Watcher. Sebastian was his name.

A youthful blonde with a Hello Kitty tote bag was beside him. She could have been his teenage daughter, all dressed in pink and black, but there was a knowing glitter in her eyes that hinted she was much older. More vampires. There was something about their presence that made the hair rise on the back of Mel's neck. Raymond muttered something unflattering and she sensed that he was hiding behind her. Neither of the new arrivals were as pale as Micah, and they were both more substantial. Mel understood that they had just feasted and was revolted.

It was probably better not to ask for details

Sebastian looked around at the Others, confident in his knowledge. "She'll go after the book first. She needs her ledger. She likes to keep score."

"And it's hidden?"

"It's safe," Micah said with authority.

Sebastian flicked a look at Micah "Not exactly. The custodian recognized what it is."

Mel dropped the glass in her surprise and it shattered on the floor between her feet. Raymond tsk'd behind her and Murray swore, but she couldn't look away from the conviction in Sebastian's gaze.

"How is that possible?" she demanded. "I thought there was a glamor on it."

"No one should be able to see the truth of the book," Micah said, as if he doubted Sebastian's assertions. "Certainly not a human. That was the whole point of choosing her."

"Well, too bad for that plan," Sebastian said. "There's more to Sylvia Fontaine than anyone guessed, and she sees through the glamor. It's only a matter of time before she realizes what it is."

"Or before she realizes where it is," Mel whispered.

Sebastian nodded, then pandemonium ruled in the bar. "We need a new plan," he said but Micah shook his head.

"I'm sure..." the leader of the coven began, but Sebastian strode away, clearly impatient.

"You're wrong," Sebastian retorted.

"And what do you care?" the blonde asked Sebastian. "You did what you were told."

"My part is not done," Sebastian hissed.

"What are you going to do?" Micah called after the other vampire.

"Take it back," Sebastian whispered at the door,

and then he was gone.

The blonde came to the bar, surveyed the wolf shifter, then smiled at Mel. "I'll have what he's having."

"You're not going after him?" the wolf shifter asked her.

"What for?"

"To defend his back."

She laughed lightly. "He prefers to be alone. We all do." Her expression turned mocking. "Unlike you, we don't run in a pack. We don't think like a hive. And we don't work in unison." She touched her beer, glanced to his and drank as the wolf shifter regarded her with disgust.

"What about the coven of mercy?"

"It's a fluid consortium," she said, much to Micah's displeasure. "I think it might be a smaller one now."

Something passed between the vampires, a current of energy so lethal that it seemed to crackle in the air between them. Mel couldn't help but notice that Micah was the first to drop his gaze.

Because he hadn't fed yet. He was weaker.

"This cannot be a good augury," Raymond whispered as the mood shifted in the bar. The Others began to argue and once again, Mel felt their union crumbling.

How and why had Micah chosen the human woman who'd been given the book? Mel wanted to know more, but Micah flickered and retreated. He was gone before she could make a sound. How had

Sebastian known to watch for the arrival of the book in Mel's apartment? If Micah had told him, then how had Micah known? Who had the fallen angel been? How had Sylvia known to come to Bones? Mel had watched Sebastian give her the book, but had thought it to be a random choice.

She had the definite sense that the vampires were running their own game and withholding a lot of information.

Maybe the vampires were even on Maeve's side.

The blonde vampire finished her beer, meeting Mel's gaze over the rim of the glass, then smiled.

Sebastian left the Others without a backward glance.

The simple truth was that when anything of importance had to be done, it was better that he do it himself. He should never have allied with Micah and the Coven of Mercy. He should never have agreed to wait to collect the book, and he should never have surrendered it to Sylvia as Micah had instructed.

Micah had no respect for magick. Micah didn't know the risks.

Sylvia needed to be defended.

At this point, the best Sebastian could do was retrieve the book and hypnotize Sylvia so that she forgot everything related to the book. It wasn't a perfect solution, but screw-ups demanded compromises.

Sebastian hated compromise.

He wasn't good at being part of a team. He'd taken care of himself for centuries, just fine. Self-sufficiency was part of what he loved about his nature, though it was convenient to hunt with Bella when he had time constraints.

He just wouldn't do that very often.

In fact, he wouldn't do it again. He was done with the coven, or would be as soon as he'd figured out what to do with the book.

First, he had to get it. That should be easy.

It felt good to run across the rooftops, although he cursed the high rise buildings that were springing up like mushrooms across the city. He liked cities with human scale, buildings that were maybe six stories high at most. Superman might be able to leap taller ones in a single bound, but Sebastian found them too ugly to test himself.

He went around them. But as the city grew, he knew that one day, the leaping he loved wouldn't even be possible.

Perish the thought that he would move to the suburbs.

He landed on the roof of the building where Sylvia lived and listened. He could hear the residents in all the units of the converted townhouse but he was most interested in the two women on the top floor.

They were both sleeping, although one was more restless than the other.

Sylvia.

He moved silently to the small terrace at the front of the building, slipping from the roof under the cover of the shadows. He couldn't descend all the way to the terrace, since there were buildings facing this one, with windows that weren't covered. He peeked down from the corner and could just barely see her face.

She frowned in her sleep, her dark brows drawn together in concern. The expression made her look vulnerable and uncertain, a combination that appealed to Sebastian's nobler impulses. Now that he had feasted, he could look at her without seeing how soft her skin was on her throat, without being so aware of the pulse of warm blood so close to the surface. Now that he had feasted, he could be a little more dispassionate in assessing her beauty.

Now that he had feasted, he could remember other sensual delights. When the thirst was upon him, it obliterated all other physical needs. The thirst was sated, and his desire for an intimate union grew.

Sylvia clutched something to her chest beneath the sheets and he guessed that it was the book. He doubted it could be pulled from her grasp without her noticing.

He'd have to wait for his moment.

Wait and watch.

Again.

She looked so vulnerable. It would be so easy to sink his teeth into her fair skin, to take her essence and her blood. She'd be safe from the dark queen then, because she'd be dead.

The very idea repelled him, which was interesting.

He wanted her to remain alive. He wanted her to continue with her dull little mortal life, as if he'd never intervened. He wanted to change the past few hours, wipe them out, not destroy her because of what he'd done. Strange how he killed mortals all the time with little concern, but this one, this one awakened his almost-forgotten sense of responsibility.

It would have been so much easier if she'd been oblivious to the book's truth.

The fact that she wasn't fed his fascination with her. She was more than an ordinary mortal and that made her worthy of his curiosity.

It made Sylvia special—and worth defending.

A taxi came down the street and Sebastian retreated to the roof, crouching beside the chimney where the shadows were deepest. He knew he should simply guard Sylvia from the roof, but the temptation was too great.

And Sebastian had never followed the rules.

It was only sensible to find out exactly what she'd seen. Yes, understanding the full extent of her memories was only sensible, because he'd have a better idea of how deeply to hypnotize her. It was flimsy, as excuses went, and he knew it. But he would take the justification for learning more about her all the same.

He took a deep breath, then slipped into Sylvia's

dreams, so smoothly that he might have even belonged there.

Ah, the red room. Sebastian smiled, knowing he could work with that.

Sylvia dreamed of the red room.

Once again, Sebastian closed the door behind himself. He leaned back against it, that seductive smile curving his lips, his eyes glowing with anticipation. Sylvia's mouth went dry and her pulse skipped.

It had been so long, but this would be worth the wait.

He said nothing at all, but surveyed her, obviously pleased by what he saw. Sylvia glanced down to find herself wearing a black satin halter dress that looked vintage. It clung to her curves like nothing she had ever chosen to wear herself. Even without a mirror, she knew the back plunged low because she could feel the pillar of the bed against her bare back. The front also had a deep vee and she could see her own cleavage. Her skin looked very pale against the black. Her hair was twisted up and her neck was bare. Long earrings brushed against her throat when she moved. She wore high heeled sandals, also black, the heels much higher than she'd ever worn before. She could feel that she was wearing stockings and a garter belt, but not much else beneath the smooth satin.

She felt seductive. Alluring. Sexy. It was an

unfamiliar sensation.

Sebastian crossed the room with leisurely steps. He moved like a panther or a predator, slowly, as if he thought she might disappear—or flee. Sylvia stayed put, although her heart raced with greater and greater speed. When he was standing right before her, his smile broadened a little. She tipped her head back to hold his gaze and his eyes were such a vivid blue that she couldn't look away. She couldn't take a breath when he lifted one hand to her throat. His fingertips brushed against her skin, his gaze following the progress of his hand as he moved it upward. He touched her earring, making it tinkle, then slid his fingertip around the curve of her ear, making her tingle. His fingers slipped into her hair, pushing the pins out of her hair so that one heavy lock tumbled loose. His fingers tightened slightly, his grip turning possessive as his hand closed around her nape. He bent closer and Sylvia tipped her head back, her lips parting as his mouth grazed her jaw. He kissed her ear so gently that she shivered, then grazed it with his teeth. Sylvia felt as if her bones were melting, and that was before his lips brushed over hers.

It was a light kiss, a promise and a tease. He did it again and she heard him chuckle when she caught her breath. She couldn't stand him being so close and not tasting her, so she straightened and leaned against him, sliding her hands around his waist. He was lean and strong, she fanned out her hands on the back of his waist before pressing herself against him. This time, he caught his breath and she glimpsed the hungry glitter in his eyes before his mouth slanted over hers in possessive demand.

His kiss was hungrier and more demanding than she'd expected, but Sylvia loved it. She kissed him back, opening her mouth to him, moaning at the expert caress of his lips and teeth and tongue. He hauled her against his chest, his desire setting her blood on fire, and his other arm locked around her waist. She arched against him, taut with need, then rubbed herself against his erection.

He inhaled sharply and backed away, taut with restraint. This time, his survey was quicker and hotter. On impulse, Sylvia unfastened the halter of the dress, baring her breasts to his view. Her nipples were dark and taut, and when he stared, throat working, she unzipped the dress and kicked it aside. He chuckled, his hand falling to the nest of curls at the top of her thighs, his gaze locking with hers as his fingers eased into her slick heat. Sylvia took a step to one side, giving him access, and gripped the post of the bed as she leaned back in surrender.

"Seductress," he murmured, but didn't seem to have an issue with that. He fell to his knees before her. His mouth closed over her and Sylvia gasped with pleasure as his tongue flicked over her clitoris. She sighed when he lifted her, placing her knees upon his shoulders, and braced herself against the bed as he ate her with leisure. Every time she approached her climax, he retreated, letting the passion build again, teasing her repeatedly with the promise of release until she heard herself beg for satisfaction. Her voice was husky and sounded strained to her own ears, as unlike her usual practical tones as could be imagined. His fingers gripped her buttocks, his demanding kiss drove her higher, and Sylvia writhed against the pleasure he was determined to give. His teeth grazed her clitoris and she cried out as the pleasure flooded through her, roaring with satisfaction.

She blinked at the sudden pounding and her eyes flew open. Her breath was short. The sheets were twisted around her, her skin slick with the patina of release, and the room smelled of her arousal. She was startled to find herself alone.

Then Celeste pounded on the ceiling beneath her once again.

Sylvia fell aback against the pillow. She'd awakened the neighbor with the sound of her release, and she'd done it all by herself.

That was a first.

Where was the book?

She panicked because it wasn't in her hand or beneath the pillow, but she found it on the floor on one side of the bed. It was open and she wondered if she imagined the little glitter of gold dust above it.

Sylvia snatched it up, noting that it was open to the page with the list of vampires, then shoved it beneath her pillow.

She really had to get some sleep.

Daylight was the bane of Sebastian's existence.

He hated it more than he hated anything in the world. Even the faintest glimmer of sunlight burned his skin and his eyes. He lingered so long with Sylvia and her seductive dreams that the sun was already cresting the horizon when he left. It was bad planning on his part. Once again, Sylvia had tempted him to change his routine and his rules.

She'd also fallen asleep on top of the book, leaving him no way to take it without awakening her. He'd been in her dreams, but would have needed to enter her apartment, as well, to claim a physical item. Better to hide the fact that he could pick the locks on her patio doors for the moment— and await a better opportunity.

The eastern sky was light when he raced across the rooftops and he knew he couldn't flee far in time. The apartment where he'd watched for the book's arrival was too distant, and probably not a good refuge anyway, given the portal to Fae in Melusine's studio. If the dark queen hadn't followed the fallen angel yet, she soon would.

Let her find Melusine alone. Mother and daughter understood each other as few others did.

He raced, ducking humans at their windows, and finally landed on the roof of the antique shop. He knocked and the door was opened immediately to him, although Rosemary's gaze was assessing. He pushed past her and shut the door.

"Micah wants to talk to you," she said.

"Micah will have to wait. I'm tired." Sebastian

eased past her and strode to the room he preferred.

It was the library, of course.

He pivoted once inside the room, met Rosemary's gaze again, then flicked the door shut with his fingertips.

He turned the key in the lock, knowing that the lock offered no real barrier to his kind. He was making a point, and he heard Rosemary move away, choosing not to challenge him.

Micah must not have a revised plan.

The blinds were already down, but he pulled the heavy drapes over the windows, too. The room was glorious in its details, the retreat of a wealthy Edwardian gentleman, and the book collection was superb.

Sebastian turned on a desk lamp with a very low wattage bulb and surveyed the glass fronted bookcases. Was there any information in this library that he could use? He was too restless to sleep and old books so often held old secrets.

He started at the top shelf in one corner, opening the doors and running his fingertip along the titles, embossed in gold on the leather covers. There had to be something here about the Fae. It would have been written by a human, but sometimes, their kind inadvertently caught hold of a truth.

CHAPTER FOUR

ylvia and Emily had a bit of a rush in the morning because they'd both slept in, but they did get to Penn Station in time for Emily's train.

They had to run.

To Sylvia's relief, Emily had missed her orgasm in the wee hours of the morning, and she didn't feel inclined to tell her friend about it. They hugged and promised to get together more often, just the way they always did, then Emily complained about her headache.

"That's what you get for ordering a drink called Name Your Poison," Sylvia said. "Twice."

"Don't say it so loud," Emily complained with a wince. Then she smiled. "Good birthday, though?"

"Great birthday, because you were here."

"And it seems to be raining men around you.

Maybe this is the year that you find the one."

"I don't need a partner."

"But a man can be more fun than another vibrator." Emily gave her another hug and turned toward the train platform. "Better conversation." She looked back from ten paces away and shrugged, her eyes twinkling. "Usually."

"I don't need conversation..."

"No. You need an orgasm!" Emily shouted and people turned to look.

"Emily!" Sylvia protested but her friend laughed, unrepentant.

And really, Sylvia didn't want her to change one bit.

Sylvia waved one last time, then checked her watch before hurrying toward work. She was passing the stationary shop at the end of the block when she spotted notebooks in the window, notebooks just like the book the waiter had given to her.

On impulse, she ducked inside to look at them. These didn't glimmer or change, no matter how much she looked at them or turned them. On impulse, she took two to the check-out.

"I can give you a better price on six," the man there joked.

"All right," Sylvia said, wondering just how often—and for how long—she'd have to defend this strange little book. She kept one in her hand and put the others in a foldable tote bag she kept in her purse for shopping. She zipped it up so no one would be able to see what was inside.

Maybe she was getting paranoid, but if someone wanted the book, they could snatch the cheap notebook out of her hand instead.

She should have felt vindicated that someone did.

Instead, Sylvia was alarmed.

It happened so fast. She was hurrying along the street to work, making her way through the crowds of people doing the same, holding tightly to the strap of her purse with one hand and the book with the other. She'd put the tote bag with the extra books on her shoulder, so that her purse was closest to her body and barricaded by the tote bag. She was right by the entrance to the subway, where people streamed down the stairs. It always made her think of lemmings, and it was a struggle to keep from being swept along with the tide.

Someone bumped her from behind on the purse side.

She glanced that way to look at the offender, and felt the book being tugged out of her other hand. By the time she looked back, she could only see a dark figure being swallowed by the crowd that flowed down to the subway station.

"Hey!" she shouted but no one paid any attention to her. She hadn't even seen the thief—he or she wore a black coat, which didn't exactly narrow the list of suspects—but she instinctively wanted to chase him or her.

She saw a flash in the crowd ahead of her, like a spark jumping from a passing train. But the tracks weren't that close. She couldn't even see the turnstiles. The crowd flowed on and she had the definite sense that her assailant couldn't be pursued, much less caught.

She still had the real book, though. She bunched her purse under her arm, holding it more tightly, and hurried into the library.

Sylvia worked in a branch of the library that was an old Carnegie building. It had been renovated to make it more accessible and the large windows made for a bright interior space. She relaxed at the sound of children, already gathered for the morning reading session with parents. She waved to the two librarians on the front desk, then dove down the stairs.

Fortunately, she worked in the archives in the basement. No one would get near her without her noticing. No one would bother her, or know if she spent a little time researching the book's contents instead of digitizing old files.

Most of the time, no one even remembered that she was here.

She shut and locked the door behind herself, glad that she'd made a habit of doing that. The head librarian had been surprised by a homeless person one night while in the archives, so had enacted the rule. There was a doorbell that any of the other librarians could ring to be let in.

Sylvia heaved a sigh of relief. The archives weren't just her domain—they were her refuge and on this day, she was glad of that. She turned on her laptop and sat down at her desk with purpose.

It was time to figure out what was so special about this book.

Sylvia started with the title.

Maeve.

An older name for Queen Mab, goddess and warrior queen of Irish origin. Maeve chose mortal champions as her consorts and made them kings—through the Great Rite of sexual union and the warrior's drinking of her mead, which may have contained menstrual blood—then discarded them when she chose another, braver, bolder or more faithful male companion. After the arrival of Christianity, this pagan goddess was reduced to a fairy queen, and depicted as being of a very small size. Her appetites remained the same, however, and her power was still said to be disproportionate to her apparent size.

It seemed unlikely to Sylvia that an ancient warrior queen would have written or kept a book, but she was prepared to consider the possibility. She opened the book, noting that it was easier to see the writing inside this time. Maybe she was getting more accustomed to turning her head just right to see it. She still couldn't understand all the script, which seemed to be in several languages, so she studied the pictures.

First were the unicorns. After several pictures,

there was a map of the world with red X's in several spots. Then there was a list of names, each of which had a dark red line through it and what had to be a date.

Was this a list of actual living unicorns?

If so, there had only been three of them.

And the dates? The red line made Sylvia doubt that the dates corresponded to sightings. No, she had to think that the unicorns had died.

Or been killed.

Assuming they'd been real in the first place. The last date was in the year 1853, and the same date was written on the first line drawing of a unicorn in the book. She'd seen it before. The last name on the list was circled with a note *"horn and harness"*.

Sylvia shivered. Did this Maeve keep trophies of creatures she'd killed?

Next was a line drawing of an elf, at least Sylvia assumed it was an elf by the points of its ears. She thought the script was in a different language than in the first section, and wondered if it was in the language of the elves. Did elves have a written language? They did in *The Lord of the Rings*, but that was fiction. Wasn't it? The list of names was much longer, but again, each one had been stroked out with that red pen and dated. The last name was circled and there was a notation *"ear"*.

That was worse than the unicorn horn.

This hunt had taken a lot longer. The dates ranged from the 1200's through 1924.

Mermaids were next and the pattern was the

same. Several illustrations, a map—this time with the X's in the oceans—a list of crossed-out and dated names—more than unicorns, fewer than elves—then the gruesome listing of the trophy beside the last one. *"Mirror and comb plus scale."*

Sylvia fanned through the book until she got to a section where the names weren't all crossed-out. Vampires. The list had been long, but there were thirteen names remaining. Micah. Rosemary. Belladonna. Sebastian....The map had thirteen bright red X's in New York, which was just weird.

Had vampires congregated in Manhattan? Had they moved to the Big Apple for some reason? Or was this the last of them, huddled together to defend themselves?

Although it was hard to think of vampires as vulnerable, the crossed-out names suggested otherwise. Maybe the vampires had just arrived. Maybe they were being hunted.

It wasn't like she could Google it.

She tipped the book, thinking that something had glimmered on the page and caught a glimpse of three words scribbled on the map beside the island of Manhattan.

Coven of Mercy.

What did that mean?

"So, Sebastian was right. You *can* see the truth of the book," a man said and Sylvia jumped. She looked at the door but it was still closed and locked. She spun to find the man standing in the shadows at the end of the aisle of filing cabinets, his arms folded across his chest. He had dark hair and dark eyes and was conservatively dressed, and so still that he was almost one with the shadows. "That defies expectation and is very inconvenient."

"How long have you been there?" she demanded. "How did you get in?"

"Long enough," he said and began to stroll toward her. "You must know that there are tiers of passageways beneath the city."

"The subway."

"More than the subway. There's a vast network. One can travel anywhere in Manhattan without ever emerging on the street." He smiled and she saw that his incisors were pointed. "Thank goodness." His skin was pale, paler than it should have been, and she felt that sense of restrained power.

The same sense she'd had when the waiter had given her the book, but without the sexual charge.

Maybe he wasn't her type.

He raised a brow. "And you can see me, which is very interesting."

"You're standing right in front of me."

"But mortals can usually only see me when they're going to die."

That wasn't good news. "Am I?"

"All mortals will die, sooner or later." His gaze slid from hers, as if he was evading the question, which wasn't the most reassuring choice.

"When?" Sylvia demanded.

"I'm not at liberty to say. It's considered bad luck, if not bad manners." His expression was rueful.

Sylvia glanced down at the book then back at him. "But you didn't expect me to be able to see you, so that's not why you're here."

He smiled, inviting her to continue.

"You're here because of the book."

He nodded.

She turned to the page on vampires and held it up. "You must be on this list."

"I'm afraid we all are."

"You mentioned Sebastian. Is he the one who gave me this book?"

"And who stood guard over you last night. You might have noticed him in your dreams."

Sylvia wasn't about to tell this stranger and vampire about her sexy dreams of Sebastian. "He's this Sebastian?" She tapped the book. "The vampire on the list?"

"There aren't any others left."

"So, this book is an inventory."

"It's a list that she's using to hunt us all."

"Why give it to me?"

"For safekeeping."

Sylvia sighed with exasperation. "Bad plan. Someone already tried to steal it."

"That won't be the last attempt."

"Then why give it to me?"

He sighed. "You weren't supposed to recognize it for what it was. That would have made it safe in your care, and you safe as its custodian."

"I don't understand."

"*She* can read the thoughts of others. Ignorance is the only thing that would have saved you, and perhaps us."

"She? You mean M—"

He moved with lightning speed, his fingertips over her mouth and his eyes filled with alarm before she could utter the name. "Do not say it aloud," he whispered, leaning over her and suddenly seeming much more frightening than before. "It's bad enough if you think it."

"But where is she?"

"Everywhere. Nowhere. She is not constrained by dimensions and realms, as we are."

"I don't understand."

"You will." He turned and walked down the aisle again. Even as she watched him, the edges of his figure seemed to soften and merge with the shadows.

"You forgot your book," she said, holding it out toward him.

"You must keep it now, for better or for worse." His serene manner infuriated Sylvia.

"You can't do this!" she protested. "If I'm in danger because of this book, then you have to take it back."

"It's too perilous and it wouldn't matter anyway. You've seen it. The memory is in your mind. You are already prey, or will become so, whether you surrender the book or not."

"I'll throw it away."

"It still won't matter."

Prey. Sylvia didn't want to be prey. "Why can't I just give it back?"

"The dark Fae do not suffer mortals to know their secrets."

"Then mortals shouldn't have their books." She dropped the book on her desk, looking at it with disgust. "This thing should have a warning label."

"Would one have stopped you from looking inside?" He seemed to be genuinely curious, which meant that Sylvia had to tell him the truth.

"No," she acknowledged. "But I would have made a choice, then. I would have known that opening the book was trouble."

He shook his head, his expression confident. "But you did know, didn't you? You knew immediately that there was something odd about it."

Sylvia nodded, because he was right.

"And you opened it all the same. Repeatedly. So you made a choice and you are part of the battle now." He turned to walk away again.

"You drop something like that and you're just going to leave? If I'm part of the battle, shouldn't I know more about the war? Shouldn't I know how to defend myself? You got me into this by giving me this book. You can't just abandon me."

He paused at the end of the aisle. "I never suggested we would." He lifted his hand, indicating her desk and Sylvia pivoted to find a card beside her keyboard. It hadn't been there before and she hadn't seen him put it there, but then, she hadn't seen him close the distance between them to stop *her* name from being uttered aloud.

"*Reliquary*," she read from the business card. There was an address that she thought was in Soho and even a website url. She looked up at him. "You run a shop?"

"Only the finest of antiquities, by appointment. Shall we say nine?" He didn't wait for a reply. He turned and rounded a corner, disappearing behind the shelf of files. She heard a slight creak, caught a whiff of dampness, and knew he was gone.

But where? Sylvia marched down the aisle, book in one hand and business card in the other. There was no sign of him. The room was long and narrow, and the only way out was back along the aisle she'd just walked or down the next one. He wasn't in either.

She remembered his comment about tunnels and scanned the walls. They were covered with bookshelves and boxes of files. The ceiling was ten feet high and she would have seen him over the shelf if he'd jumped. She dropped to her knees and ran her hands across the floor. She couldn't see the trapdoor right away, but she felt it. It was tiled to match the cheap linoleum used on the archive floor, but slightly higher. As she ran her fingers along the ridge, it sank down to be level again.

Just as if it wasn't there.

But it was and she knew it now. Sylvia couldn't feel a clasp or a handle, but maybe he'd left it open when he arrived.

Maybe the archives weren't as safe as she'd

thought.

There was more than one way to keep a trapdoor closed. She dragged a filing cabinet over the trap door with considerable effort, then looked at the card again.

He hadn't told her his name, but he was on that list.

Before she could open the book again and consider the possibilities, the doorbell rang.

"Give me a minute!" she shouted and ran back to the computer. She wiped the browser history, pulled up an archive record, and shoved the book and card into her purse. Then she went to the door, opened it and smiled at her co-worker. "Sorry. I dropped a file behind that filing cabinet and was right in the middle of moving it out from the wall."

Sylvia went home to eat before going to the antique shop. She also wanted to talk to her aunt. She was so busy thinking about the book and the implications of having it in her possession that she strode down the street with her head down.

She ran right into Caleb.

It was a spectacular collision, one that sent her purse and tote bag skyward and their contents scattering. Caleb had been carrying a burlap sack of peanuts in the shell, which was large enough to obstruct his vision. It split, raining peanuts all over the sidewalk. They both fell down and stared at each other in surprise. Caleb was dressed for work, wearing a dark blue security guard uniform. He looked trim and neat.

His gaze slipped over her and he smiled as Sylvia straightened her glasses.

"I'm sorry..."

"No, I'm sorry..."

They exchanged apologies as they both crouched down to pick everything up. The notebooks were scattered all over the place, most of them splayed open, and Caleb stacked them up with care, smoothing the bent corners. Sylvia's purse had apparently exploded, because her wallet and keys and everything else was loose. She thought the book was gone, but then saw Caleb put it back in her purse with her wallet.

She exhaled in relief, and tried to help him gather the peanuts again. The burlap bag wasn't going to hold all of them, now that it was split, so she offered her tote bag to him.

"But your books..."

"I can carry the little stack upstairs. It's not a big deal. You'll have a much harder time with ten pounds of loose peanuts."

He smiled ruefully. "You're right. I offered to pick them up for the circus today, but they probably aren't expecting me to bring them individually."

They laughed together and got the peanuts into either the end of the burlap bag that was still intact or Sylvia's tote bag. Caleb stood then offered his hand to Sylvia, helping her to get up. There was a warm glint of appreciation in his eyes, one that made her very aware of the strength of his hand.

"Thanks for your help," he said. "I'm sorry I didn't see you coming." He picked up the stack of notebooks and handed them to her.

"I wasn't looking where I was going either."

"Are you sure you're okay with those?"

"They're just notebooks. I'm find." Sylvia smiled and Caleb smiled, and time seemed to stop. When a window high overhead creaked open, she realized that they were standing and staring at each other like besotted idiots.

And that Celeste in 4F was watching.

"I hope you have a good night at work," Sylvia said, thinking it was a lame comment but not knowing what else to say.

He shrugged. "I'll settle for uneventful. One of the snakes got out of its pen last night."

"Oh. Did you find it again?"

He nodded. "When the patron in the third row screamed."

"I guess she got more thrills than she expected."

"I guess so." He smiled again and Sylvia could have stood with him all day. A gust of wind made her skirt swirl and sent a cloud of dead leaves spinning down the street. Caleb leaned over to the big window that was in the front of his apartment.

"Be quiet tonight, Loki," he said, although Sylvia couldn't see the dog. "I'll be back soon."

Sylvia had gone to the gate that blocked the front patio from the street. There were narrow steps there that went down to the door beneath the main door to the building. Once this lower level had been the kitchen, storage and some servant quarters, but now it was Eithne's office in the front and her own apartment at the back. Sylvia wanted to ask her about Caleb moving in so quickly.

"How are you settling in?" she asked.

"Well enough. It doesn't take long to unpack in two hundred square feet."

"It's not a lot of space for you and Loki."

He grinned and looked suddenly younger. "They offered me a trailer at the circus. This is luxurious in comparison." He waved two fingers at her and turned to leave. "I'd better get going so I'm not late."

"You work at night?"

"This circus is only open at night." He smiled and continued down the street, heading toward Stuyvesant Park. She'd have to look at that flyer again and see where the circus was located.

Funny how she hadn't heard that there was one around.

Sylvia knocked on Eithne's door but there was no answer. That didn't surprise her: her aunt seldom answered the door. She used her key and locked the door again behind herself. "Aunt Eithne!" she shouted, not wanting to surprise her. ""It's me!" Her heels clicked on the marble floor as she walked down the corridor. There was an office on this floor, directly under Caleb's apartment and the same size, then Eithne's apartment was at the back, under Rachel's. The big difference was that Eithne had the patio and backyard to herself. 2B and 3B had small balconies but no one came into the garden except Eithne and Sylvia.

The door to Eithne's apartment was open, as it often was, and Sylvia smelled soup. Lentil soup, maybe with a bit of bacon or ham. She could smell pastry, too, and her stomach grumbled with predictable enthusiasm.

Eithne made the best quiche Sylvia had ever tasted. When it was hot out of the oven, it was divine.

She tapped on the door but saw that the door to the garden was open, even though the evening was already getting cool. She noticed that the table was set for two for dinner as she passed through the apartment, and saw the quiche cooling on the counter. She leaned over it and took a deep breath. Leek with ham and little tomatoes baked on top. Her stomach reminded her that she'd skipped lunch.

She found her aunt in the garden. Eithne was wearing the blue linen apron she always put on to garden, the one with the big pockets in front. She was cutting a bouquet of dahlias and chrysanthemums. They were in rich autumn colors of burgundy and gold, and she was turning the makeshift arrangement in her hands, as if deciding whether to cut more. Her silver hair was tugged back into a ponytail and Sylvia wondered again just how old her aunt was. She was slender and tall, and so active that it was hard to believe she was older than Sylvia.

Eithne looked up and smiled in welcome. "This will be the last of it, I expect."

"They're pretty, though." Sylvia kissed her aunt's cheek.

"They are. Are you hungry?"

"I don't want to interfere if you're having company..."

"The company I'm having is you," Eithne said firmly. "I knew you would come tonight and I knew you'd have questions. We might as well eat while I answer them."

It wasn't the first time that her aunt had anticipated her, but on this night, Sylvia wondered at it. Maybe she came honestly by this ability to see auras—or whatever they were.

"How did you know I'd come?"

"Because there's a new tenant and I didn't tell you about it. You always come to check on things like that." It sounded reasonable, but Sylvia had the sense that it was half an explanation.

Maybe she was just getting into the habit of looking for things that weren't there.

Eithne led Sylvia back to the kitchen. She opened a bottle of wine and poured two glasses, giving one to Sylvia before she arranged the flowers. She frowned as she worked. "I didn't tell you because I didn't know."

"You must have known."

"I did but not with enough time. One minute, Carlo was moving out with no notice and we were arguing about his deposit, and the next, there was

Caleb on the doorstep. He had an answer to every question and looked so reliable." Eithne pursed her lips, her frustration with tenants showing. "It was almost as if it had been arranged."

Sylvia didn't like the sound of that. "Arranged? Who would arrange that?"

"I don't know, but that was the sense I had." Eithne shook her head, then brought the flowers to the table. "But then I thought I was being silly. Here was a perfectly good tenant, a nice man with a job and perfect credentials, one who sleeps in the daytime and works at night. It's not that easy to find good tenants so I decided not to turn away such a good choice."

"Why did Carlos move out?"

"It was odd. He said there was a ghost and he wouldn't stay one minute longer." Eithne tasted the soup, then nodded before turning up the heat on the element. "No one has ever complained about a ghost in 2F." She wagged a finger. "4B, now, that's another story."

"Aren't ghosts supposed to haunt the place they died?"

"If they have unfinished business."

"So, did anyone ever die in 2F?"

"No." Eithne put down her spoon. "That's the curious thing. There can't be a ghost there, and I'm skeptical about the one in 4B, too."

"Someone could have died there before you owned the house," Sylvia noted and Eithne's gaze slid away from hers.

"Mmm," she said, even more noncommittal than usual, and she changed the subject. "Do you want to go upstairs to change or anything before we eat?"

Sylvia agreed, then headed out of the apartment to climb the stairs. She couldn't help feeling that she'd been dismissed for a moment, and that Eithne wasn't telling her all of the truth.

Could her aunt be hiding something from her?

She frowned and hurried up the stairs. Once in her apartment, she hung up her coat and washed her face, then changed to jeans and a sweater. On impulse, she scattered the notebooks around her apartment, hiding each one in a different place. She left one on the couch, as if she'd been reading it, and tugged on a favorite big cardigan. She tucked the book from her purse into the pocket, finding the weight of it reassuring. Eithne's place could be a bit damp, especially if she left open the doors to the garden—which she would—so her aunt would never realize Sylvia had brought a book along.

Eithne might have secrets, but she wasn't the only one.

CHAPTER FIVE

he key, the key, the key. How much would Sebastian do to retrieve his key?

A lot, it was clear.

Even more than he'd expected, apparently.

He cursed the day that he had ever let a Fae put a curse upon his key, the key that opened his ultimate sanctuary, the key that Fae had ultimately stolen and that Micah had somehow found. The key opened the one lock Sebastian couldn't pick.

By his own scheme with the curse, which made that fact even more bitter.

He'd lost the argument with Micah because of the fucking key and his need to reclaim it. And now he was an escort service.

Not even the fun kind.

Sebastian seethed as he made his way to Sylvia's apartment again. He wasn't a messenger boy. He wasn't Micah's slave.

But he might as well have been as long as Micah had his key.

He really had to figure out a way to steal it back and cut himself free of all these obligations and responsibilities. When he got the key and was back inside his sanctuary, he might not ever leave it again. He'd figure out a way to tempt some unfortunate inside at regular intervals so the thirst didn't destroy him.

First, the key.

He needed something to negotiate with, which meant he had to get the book back.

Why had Micah chosen Sylvia? Of all the mortals in Manhattan, it defied belief that Micah had chosen the one, possibly the only, who could see the truth of the book. It seemed like ridiculously bad luck.

Maybe she hadn't been someone who could see its truth before she got the book. Before she touched it, or opened it. Maybe Sylvia's psychic abilities had been triggered by possession of the book. Now there was an interesting notion. Maybe any mortal who held the book would be able to see its truth.

Huh. That would be bad luck, but of a different kind. An inescapable kind.

Sebastian wouldn't have put it past her to have included a neat little trick like that in the glamor defending the book.

If that was even possible. One difficulty with having an enormous respect and thus a wariness of magick was that Sebastian didn't actually know what was possible with magick and what was not.

He still didn't want to learn.

Sebastian landed lightly on the terrace behind Sylvia's kitchen and inhaled deeply. How he hated the smell of werewolf. The scent of any shifter, actually, made him recoil in disgust. He halfway agreed with Maeve that there was something deeply unnatural about the ability to change physical forms.

It was a revolting power.

He looked into the apartment, halfway surprised that Sylvia wasn't home yet. Then he saw her coat on the back of a chair, her purse and shoes beside it. She'd been home and left, then. He wondered where she'd gone, then heard women's laughter from below. There were lights in the garden at the back of the house, illuminating the patio.

No, they were candles, flickering in the evening air.

He crouched down as two people came out of the house, each carrying a wine glass. He smelled blood and perfume and vulnerability, a combination so delicious that it almost made him dizzy. It certainly heightened his protective urges. The thirst was only a low hum of awareness, or his urges might have been predatory. He'd sated himself the night before and didn't need to drink daily. His awareness of the women and their mortality was like a little buzz of interest, one that got an extra kick when he recognized Sylvia's voice.

She flicked a glance skyward and he retreated quickly, hearing her make a comment about the first sliver of the moon high overhead.

Had she sensed his presence?

Or had that glance just been a coincidence?

Sebastian was skeptical of coincidence.

He leaned against the wall, arms folded across his chest, and listened to their conversation. This plant and that plant. Boring, boring, boring. They would all be dead in five, ten, forty years, the blink of a proverbial eye. This building would likely be rubble in twenty years, replaced by one of those towers. Maybe Manhattan itself would sink into the ocean. How quaint it was that mortals cared so much about time.

What did Sylvia hope for her future? What did she dream about—besides him? Sebastian recalled the more interesting details of the night before and he found himself smiling in the darkness.

Worse, he recognized that he was becoming interested in Sylvia.

There was no future in that.

If she fantasized about him, though, he might be drawn back to her, again and again.

What if Sylvia was a pawn in Maeve's game? What if he had been targeted by the dark queen? Sebastian straightened at the thought. It had been sobering to see his name inscribed inside the book the one time he had looked. He had no intentions of ever dying, and he certainly wasn't going to risk his future defending a mortal. He might as well lay down his existence for an insect or a garden weed. Humans were a food supply, no more and no less, and becoming interested in them was a huge mistake.

That had been, after all, one of the first lessons he'd ever learned.

The second had been that relying upon anyone else of any kind was an even bigger mistake.

But he had to maintain his alliance with Micah until he got his key back.

Sylvia, however, was another thing.

He had to guard her and the book, by Micah's order, but he didn't have to feed her sexual fantasies, as intriguing and pleasurable as they might be.

The quickest solution might be to frighten her.

Sebastian didn't think it would be hard to do. She was a librarian who lived a sheltered and solitary life, one who thought trying a new restaurant was a great adventure.

It would take him moments, and make his life vastly simpler.

Theo was sure that his legs were going numb but he didn't dare fidget. Rox was finishing the tattoo on his back, and they'd agreed on a longer session since her shop, Imagination Ink, was quiet on a Sunday. He'd been ready for the persistent burn of the tattoo gun, but not for the ache from sitting in the same position for so long.

It also gave him time to think about how different Manhattan felt to him on this visit. It seemed crowded to him in a way that was entirely new.

"Almost done," Rox said, giving his shoulder a wipe. "Just a bit more detail in this eye."

Theo bowed his head and tried to ignore the tingling in his toes. He heard footsteps in the hall and knew that Niall was coming to join them before he even caught the scent of the other, older, dragon shifter. Both Theo and Niall were *Pyr*, but Niall had already found and won his human mate, Rox. Seeing them together always made Theo yearn for the spark of his own firestorm. He knew he was still young in *Pyr* terms, but he felt the absence of a lover and partner in his life.

Niall and Rox's sons made Theo long for a family, too. They had two sets of twins: Kyle and Nolan were eight while Ahern and Ruark were four.

"Are you admitting defeat?" Rox asked in a teasing voice and Theo smiled.

"Ahern and Ruark are having a nap," Niall said, then two more pairs of footsteps sounded.

"Cool!" Kyle said with enthusiasm.

"When do I get one?" Nolan demanded.

"When you're eighteen and don't ask me to do it," Rox said. "I think you're perfect just the way I made you."

The boys protested, then Niall suggested they get the sketchbooks that Rox kept in the shop for them. Within moments, they were at the table in the main room of the shop, drawing their own dragons. Theo smiled at the sound of them conferring. He'd often admired how they worked together. Maybe it was a twin thing, but Kyle always did the wings on their dragons, and Nolan always did the teeth.

"How's it going?" Niall returned and came to stand beside Rox. He didn't say anything more for a moment, and Theo might have been worried if Rox hadn't already given him several chances to look in the mirror. She'd done the outline and colored the dragon on his previous visits to Manhattan, but today, she'd been adding flames in the background. "That's really something, Rox," Niall said finally. "I think it might be your best dragon ever."

"You're my best dragon ever," she replied and Theo smiled.

"Carnelian and gold, just like Theo's own dragon form," Niall said with approval. "Those flames look amazing behind him. I like the illusion of him bursting forth."

"A portrait in a way," Rox agreed.

"Dragon out of hell," Theo said, then winced as the tattoo gun burned again. "Hey, Niall, does the city feel different to you?"

"Different how?"

"I don't know. As if the shadows are full of...something."

"Maybe you just need more sleep," Niall suggested. "The shadows seem exactly the same to me." Theo didn't say more, but he couldn't shake his feeling that something had changed.

Much less his misgivings about that.

"Okay, there are flames in his eyes now, too." Rox gave his back a wipe. "Come have a look." She gave him a hand mirror, then urged him toward the big mirror on the wall.

Even though Theo had seen the dragon already and guessed what the rest would look like, he was amazed to see it on his back. The flames and the dragon looked like they were surging out of a wound on his back, as if he'd been sliced open and the dragon had been set free.

Which was pretty much what it was like to be *Pyr.*

"It totally rocks." He handed the mirror back to her and gave her a hug. She was tiny and he was careful not to crush her—even though he knew she was fierce enough to have helped Niall defeat shadow dragons and to be the mother of two sets of twins. "Thanks so much."

"I want to take pictures when it's healed," she said.

"No problem."

She turned him around and considered her work. "It really is great. You owe me so big," she teased and Theo laughed.

"Which means you have something specific in mind."

Rox raised a brow and pulled a flyer out of the back pocket of her jeans. "The boys brought this home." She gave him an intent look and Niall's lips thinned.

It was a flyer for a circus. Theo took it with surprise and read the back. "A circus? In New York?"

"I know. It's weird," Niall said. "That's why we shouldn't patronize it."

Rox turned to face her partner. "Circuses have always provided havens for those who don't fit conveniently into society's expectations."

"Circuses have always taken advantage of those people," Niall replied. "And exploited them for financial gain."

"The tattooed lady," Rox said, her voice hardening.

"The snake man," Niall said, shaking his head with disgust.

"The bearded lady," Rox countered.

"The dog-faced boy," Niall said.

"You of all people should understand what it means not to fit in..." Rox began.

Niall interrupted her. "And I understand what it is to be exploited. When I was a boy, my father took us to the circus. I'll never forget it. It was awful. I wanted to set all the animals free. They were so sick and sad."

"Your father's been dead for two hundred years," Rox pointed out. "Conditions in circuses have changed."

"Have they?" Niall glared at her and she glared back.

Theo cleared his throat. "Let me guess. The boys

want to go, but you want to be sure it'll be a positive experience for them."

"The boys are out of luck," Niall said flatly. "We'll go to the museum."

"The boys might learn something about tolerance if they go," Rox countered. She smiled at Theo. "Would you go and check it out for us? It's not in a great area or I'd go myself..."

"And you'd be inclined to see what you want to see," Niall said.

"You need an impartial judge," Theo said, recognizing the truth. "I'll go."

"You really don't have to," Niall said.

"You've made me kind of curious." Theo glanced down at the times. "Hey, they're open Sundays and I've got no plans. I'll go tonight."

"Thank you!" Rox said and gave him another hug. "Now, let's see what we can scare up for dinner. I'm starving."

The last thing Sylvia felt like doing after having dinner with Eithne was going out, much less to meet with a coven of vampires in an antique shop. A good British mystery series viewed from her couch while enjoying a hot cup of herbal tea seemed like a better idea. The meal had been delicious and she'd eaten a little more than she should have, but then, she hadn't had lunch. Even though she'd had only one glass of wine, she felt a little bit sleepy as she climbed the stairs.

She didn't see anybody but she heard the other tenants as she climbed the stairs—well, except Caleb, who had gone to work. His dog must have been asleep because 2F was quiet. Maybe the ghost was asleep, too. Sylvia smiled at Eithne's doubts. Maybe the ghost had just been an excuse for Carlos to get out of the lease.

Rachel in 2B was at her piano, playing scales. Sonia in 3B was quiet, but then, she was always quiet. She might still be at work at the fitness club. If she was home, she did yoga or knit while listening to audiobooks. Sylvia thought she could hear the keyboard in 3F, which meant Ethan was at his computer. He was a student who did day trading, apparently with success. The only sound Ethan made was when he forgot himself and sang along with the music on his headphones.

Sylvia heard the sewing machine in 4B along with the quiet sound of an interview on the radio. Eliza was a textile artist and fan of NPR. Sylvia felt Celeste watching her through the peephole of her door at 4F and had no doubt that notes were being made on her activities. If there had ever been a murder at the house, Celeste would be the one with full records of comings and goings. Sylvia wondered if Celeste had fabricated a story about her noisy orgasm the night before and smiled with the certainty that there was no way her neighbor's story came close to the truth.

Sylvia sighed with relief when she reached her floor, not meaning to do so. It was a long climb, one that added to her desire to stay home.

She supposed it would be a bad idea to stand up a coven of vampires.

She sensed the difference as soon as she opened the door and paused on the threshold, looking. Someone had been in her apartment. Things weren't moved very much but there was a scent in the air that hadn't been there before.

Was the intruder still there?

Sylvia listened, but couldn't hear a thing. She took a step inside, closed the door behind herself and leaned against it, looking. Then she flicked on the overhead light.

Again, it seemed as if everything was as it should be.

Then she noticed that the book she'd left on the couch was gone.

She crossed the floor in a hurry, checking behind and beneath the couch. It was gone, and she knew she'd left it there. But the door had still been locked. She scanned the living room, seeking some sign of a break-in and spotted all of the other books neatly lined up on her kitchen counter. She nearly jumped out of her skin when she saw a man in her kitchen, watching her.

Sebastian.

He was leaning in the back corner, the darkest one, and absolutely motionless. His eyes could have been lit with blue fire and his lips were drawn to a thin line. He shouldn't have been allowed to wear a leather jacket and jeans. He looked very James Dean but darker and more dangerous, not just because of his tight black T-shirt.

"How did you get in here?" Her voice was breathless, the details of her dream flooding her thoughts with incredibly bad timing. She knew she was blushing and wished it would stop. She hoped he didn't know anything about her dream, and told herself it was impossible that he could.

Then he smiled so knowingly that she knew he did. "Does it matter?"

"Yes, it does. I'd like to be sure no one else can break into my apartment."

"Then you should have better locks."

"Thank you very much for that advice." She felt her eyes narrow. "So, you found the books, but not *the* book."

"I found a lot of cheap notebooks. I assume you have *the* book."

Sylvia put her hand in her pocket, resting it on top of the book.

He gestured to the books on the counter. "What are these about?"

"Decoys." Sylvia approached the kitchen counter but Sebastian didn't move. His gaze was fixed on her lips, which made her self-conscious—actually, remembering her dream and his role in it was what was making her self-conscious. She cleared her throat. "I bought a dozen of them this morning. One was stolen from me almost right away."

"By whom?"

"I don't know. It was this morning, on my way

to work. I kept it in my hand and put the real one in my purse."

"And the thief took the decoy?"

Sylvia nodded. "He or she ran into the subway. I didn't get a good look because it was crowded, but there was this little flash of light afterward." She looked at Sebastian but he dropped his gaze, feeding her sense that he was hiding something from her.

"Interesting." He perched on the stool in the kitchen. "Someone who couldn't tell the difference tried to retrieve the book."

"Who exactly can see the difference?"

"Anyone who can see past the glamor placed on it." He raised a hand. "The really interesting question is why you can do that."

"Can't everyone?"

"No. That would be the point of the glamor."

He was studying her so intently that Sylvia's blush deepened. When had she last had such a gorgeous man in her apartment? She had no idea how to deal with this unfamiliar situation—much less with him.

How did he remember her dream?

Why was he back?

What did he want?

He turned to study the few potted herbs on her counter. They were half-dead and she wished she'd done something about them, even though she hadn't been expecting company. "I'm supposed to escort you to Reliquary," he said, as if he had heard the questions in her thoughts. "It's not my best trait, following orders, and I'm not one to be inclined to take much responsibility for my actions, but you appear to be challenging expectations in more ways than one."

"Why doesn't that sound like a good thing?"

"It's not. I like my pleasures uncomplicated. I like my life uncomplicated."

"Then you shouldn't have given me the book."

He grimaced. "That's what comes of following orders. Everything goes to shit."

Sylvia folded her arms across her chest. "I don't think things are going to shit."

"Wait for it."

"Why don't you tell me what you know?"

"Why should I?"

"Ever since you gave me this book, things have been odd. I've been robbed. Twice. I've had vivid dreams."

He smiled.

"Twice."

His smile faded abruptly. "What other dream did you have?"

"I think I had a visitation of some kind. Someone called from the book, demanding its return."

He straightened, his apparent indifference dismissed. He was avidly interested now, his gaze unswerving and unblinking. "And?"

"And Micah turned up at my job today to introduce himself."

His eyes narrowed. "You could see him?"

Sylvia nodded. "Does that mean I'm going to die?"

He waved a hand. "Of course you are. You're mortal."

"I mean, soon."

"It's all relative, isn't it? If you lived to be a hundred, I'd think that was soon."

Sylvia sank down onto a stool. "You don't screw around when someone asks you for the truth, do you?"

Impatience flickered across his features. "I don't screw around, period. I do what I want, when I want, where I want, with whom I want."

"Unless you're doing what Micah tells you to do."

He winced. "Touché. Desperate times, etc. Shall we go?"

"No. Not yet. The book is important. It's filled with lists and maps. I want to know what it all means."

"Careful what you wish for," he whispered.

"I'm ready. Tell me the real risk. Am I going to die?"

He raised a brow.

Sylvia clarified, her tone impatient. "Am I going to die soon, in my terms, and because of the book?"

"I'm not a fortuneteller."

"Tell me the risk. Don't be evasive."

He crossed the room in that insanely quick way, suddenly appearing right in front of her. He bent down and Sylvia couldn't look away from the intense blue of his eyes. His voice dropped to a seductive murmur, but his words weren't seductive at all. "The real risk is that Maeve will find you and her book, that she will obliterate or maybe curse you to retrieve her property, and that then she will continue to exterminate all of the Others in the world."

"Why?" Sylvia whispered.

"She considers only Fae and humans to be pure. All of the Others are half-breeds, by her accounting, part Fae and part human, and thus abominations." He opened his hand, inviting her to answer. "And the title of the book is...?"

"Her Book of Beasts."

"Beasts," he agreed with a nod.

"Why should I care about Others?"

He tilted his head to study her. "What makes you believe that she will stop once the half-breeds are gone? If she wants Fae to be ascendant or alone on this earth, then humans will be next. It's an inevitable and logical progression."

Sylvia's heart chilled. "You're not fighting for humans. Not you."

"I am a little." He smiled and bared his pointed teeth. "I do have appetites, after all."

Sylvia had to look away. "About last night..."

"I wanted to know how much you knew about the book, but I was...distracted." How could his voice be so low and so sultry? How could just his voice make her shivery and hot in all the places that counted?

She would not think about his tongue and what it could do.

"Is that typical?"

"No. It's been quite a while since I indulged other appetites."

"But you didn't indulge yours last night." She dared to look up at him, only to find that hunger in his eyes again.

He smiled. "Oh, there was a certain satisfaction to be had in the proceedings."

"Were you really there? Or were you in my dream?"

"Does it matter?"

"Well, yes. I want to know if you broke into my apartment, or if you were vandalizing my mind..."

"You invited me," he said curtly. "I don't know where that room is and I don't know why you have a vision of us being there."

"Is it real?"

"You tell me."

Sylvia exhaled. "This is all new to me."

"Don't worry. You probably won't have long to try to figure it out."

"Thank you very much." She supposed it wasn't a surprise that his answer was consistent with Micah's. "So, what happens now?"

"We go to Reliquary to confer."

"No, between you and me."

"It would be stupid for anything to happen between you and me," he said so softly that Sylvia looked at him. There was a threat in his tone and in his posture. "You know what I am. You know what I need. You know that stories between your kind and my kind do not end well for the member of your kind."

"You don't seem very scary right now."

"I have fed. The thirst is sated, for the moment, but it will return." He opened his mouth, displaying his teeth to her a little, and waited until she shivered. "And when it returns, Sylvia Fontaine, if I am still commanded to. guard you, you would be clever to ensure that you don't tempt me in any way. I am volatile and impulsive when the thirst burns. The thirst compels me to actions that there is no time to regret."

"That must be inconvenient."

"It is the root of my current, very unsatisfactory, situation." His eyes blazed. "Do not— I repeat—do not fuck with me."

Sylvia swallowed and eased a little further away. "You're trying to scare me."

"I hope, for your sake, that I'm succeeding." He leaned over the chair, bracing one hand on each arm and trapping her there. "If not, let me make myself perfectly clear. If you summon me again with a dream like the one you had last night, if you do it when the thirst is burning, I will eat more than you expect and you will never awaken again."

"Can't you turn people to vampires?"

He straightened and spun away. "Just because something is possible doesn't mean it should be done."

"Have you ever turned anyone?"

He glared at her, his eyes as cold as ice. "Never. And I never will."

"Why not?"

"Because those a vampire turns are bound to him or her forevermore, and I want to be alone more than anything in the world."

"Why?"

"Because my black heart is filled with hate." His tone was mocking and she didn't know if he was making fun of himself or her question.

"But you're allied with Micah."

"At this point in time, it's the best way of looking out for number one. With any luck, that will not last."

"And so, the book must be defended and the enemy defeated."

"And they say humans are intellectually challenged." This time, she had no doubt that he was mocking her and she braced herself for whatever he was going to say. "There is an alternative." His voice was low and silky again, and she intuitively distrusted him.

"Which is?"

"The book can be reclaimed and your memory...deleted."

"Deleted? But Micah said there was no point..."

"Because Micah has no understanding and less respect for magick. It could be done, but you would forget everything." He shrugged. "It might not be enough, though."

"So I could give you the book, agree to have my memory wiped, but still be hunted down and killed by her."

"It would come as a surprise to you."

"No. Unequivocably no." Sylvia stood up, shedding her cardigan and getting a leather jacket instead. She tugged on her boots then took the book out of the sweater pocket. She could feel Sebastian waiting and watching, and was keenly aware of his impatience. That made her impatient. He had to know that she couldn't move in the blink of an eye. "Don't you want to know what she said through the book last night?"

"Of course."

"She demanded its return. She made threats."

"But she didn't appear?"

Sylvia shook her head and watched him consider that.

"Interesting. So, she doesn't know exactly where it is, but she's trying to summon it." Before Sylvia could ask for more detail, he moved to the patio door. "We have to go. Bring it."

"Not that way!"

"This is the only way that I'll go."

"I thought you were going to escort me on the street."

"You thought wrong."

"I can't climb across rooftops..."

"Then you'll have to rely upon my help." The prospect seemed to amuse him.

"You'll probably drop me."

"You needn't work so hard to tempt me."

Sylvia took a book from the counter, one that had been in the kitchen drawer, and gave it to him. "It's your turn to be bait," she said, her tone cross. "Don't expect me to cry if you get hurt."

He chuckled, surprised into it. "I won't. There is more to you than meets the eye." He eased closer, his gaze dropping to her lips, and Sylvia held her breath, thinking he might give her a real kiss, one that she could compare to the dream one.

Instead, his gaze fell to the book in her hand and he frowned. "I thought that one was the book," he said softly.

Sylvia lifted the book to study it, her heart sinking as she realized it was just a notebook. She looked at the notebook Sebastian held, then lunged for the counter and the books remaining there. She knew immediately but picked each one up and turned it over, just to be sure.

"It's gone," she told him, horror in her tone.

"Such an excellent custodian," he muttered as her thoughts flew.

"Caleb!" she whispered in realization.

"What?"

"The guy who moved into 2F this morning, with his dog, Loki. He bumped into me when I was coming home. My purse and tote bag spilled and the bag of peanuts he had broke. He picked up the books for me. He put one back in my purse and I thought it was the one that fell out of it."

"Fucking werewolves," Sebastian snarled and

spun, striding to the door to the terrace. "And he names his so-called dog Loki. How moronic is that?"

"There's nothing so-called about his dog. I heard it last night."

"But did you see it at the same time you could see him?"

Sylvia blinked. "I heard them both."

Sebastian shook his head, apparently despairing of the feeble intellectual power of humans. His eyes were blazing when he met her gaze. "Are you coming or not?"

"You said werewolves?"

"I said werewolves. There is a werewolf living in 2F. Call him whatever you want. Call his so-called dog whatever you want, but I would suggest that invoking an old deity known for making trouble is a really bad idea."

"I guess it would be, if you believe in that sort of thing."

"What exactly will it take to convince you?"

Sylvia smiled. "Point taken." Her expression seemed to startle Sebastian, because he blinked and stared at her for a moment, then indicated the terrace again. "Are you coming tonight?"

"Of course, I'm coming. I'm the one who knows where Caleb is."

She should have been getting used to that lightning quick movement, but Sylvia gasped when Sebastian was suddenly right before her again. His gaze bored into hers. "Where?" His voice was a low growl and it made her shiver.

It also made her want to kiss him again.

That had to be a bad idea.

"He works at the circus." Sylvia reached out and plucked the flyer that Caleb had given her earlier off the counter. "Here."

CHAPTER SIX

he *Circus of Wonders* apparently moved locations with some regularity. The flyer listed half a dozen locations with dates. Sylvia headed downstairs to get a cab to Tompkins Square Park, the current location, and Sebastian followed her with some reluctance.

"I don't like cabs," he complained.

"You don't like much of anything," she countered, which wasn't exactly unfair.

Someone moved behind the door of 4F and Sebastian glared at the door. "Not true. I like many things."

"Like?"

"Pleasure. Books. Privacy."

Sylvia flicked a glance over her shoulder at him. "Should I be worried that we have that list in common?"

"No, because another thing I don't like is humans."

"Don't put too much of a gloss on it," Sylvia muttered.

"Do you want me to lie to you?"

"No, actually, I don't. But you could try to be a little bit diplomatic."

"It's a waste of time and energy. It's much simpler just to say what you mean." He ducked past her and opened the door to the front steps and she stopped to look at him in surprise.

"Suddenly, you're a gentleman?"

"Old habits die hard."

"I guess so." Sylvia stepped into the night. There was a cab moving slowly down the street and she raised her hand. "All right. I'll play. I'd call you a pompous, critical, and annoying man, except that you're a vampire."

"I knew you liked me," he said on impulse and swept open the door of the cab.

She laughed.

He smiled. Their gazes met for an electric moment that made him almost reconsider his assumptions about humans. Then she shook her head and got into the cab.

It smelled so strongly of humans that Sebastian had to hold his breath.

"You're glittering," Sylvia whispered.

He gave her an intent look, not wanting to risk making a reply, and she laughed in the most enchanting way.

Fortunately, the cab driver wasn't chatty and the park wasn't far. Sylvia paid, making Sebastian aware of his lack of modern currency. He apologized and held the door for her again. "I don't have any cash," he said.

"I'll guess you don't have credit or debit cards either."

"No."

The circus had taken over one corner of the park. There was a large red and white striped tent, strung with flickering lights. A pair of clowns were checking tickets at the opening, and a woman in tights with a ringleader's top hat was selling tickets at a small counter. There were other booths in a circle outside the tent: Sebastian saw a fortune-teller and a magician, as well as several games of skill—which were undoubtedly rigged—between the small crowd of humans who found such pathetic spectacles entertaining. The werewolf was pacing the perimeter with a few of his fellows but hadn't seen Sebastian and Sylvia yet. It was dark enough that his skin didn't itch, but that wouldn't last.

"You said he was a werewolf," Sylvia said softly.

"Because he is."

"How do you know?"

Sebastian touched the tip of his nose.

She nodded, apparently disappointed. "Oh, I thought maybe you saw the auras, too." She continued toward the werewolf, as if she could just ask him to return her stolen book.

Sebastian seized her arm and tugged her to a halt. "What auras?" he hissed.

She held his gaze. "You don't see them at all?"

"What auras?"

She frowned. "I saw them for the first time at the bar."

"Bones."

"Yes. It was like a ghost behind and above some of the people there. The hostess had a raven. The bartender had a green dragon with a long tail. You have a red glow, like pulsing neon. And Caleb has a white wolf."

Sebastian inhaled sharply. "You can see their true nature," he whispered. "And that only started when you got to Bones?"

Sylvia nodded. "Is that important?"

"I don't know. I don't like it." He noticed her expression. "I'll add it to my list." She smiled and would have continued, but he kept a hand on her elbow. "Look now," he invited. "Look at all these people and tell me if any of them have these auras."

Sylvia looked. "Caleb, of course. Actually, all of the security guys have wolves, but they're not all white. That little girl over there has pulsing red like you."

Bella. What was she doing here? When Sebastian glanced her way, she ducked into the big tent, as if she hadn't seen him.

"The woman in the top hat has little demon's horns. That guy, the one buying a ticket from her now, he has a gold dragon."

Sebastian straightened and inhaled. Demon. Weredragon. He wanted to growl in exasperation. Anything but one of the *Pyr*. He hated weredragons more than he hated werewolves.

"And that guy," Sylvia said, pointing to a tall blond guy. "His is flashing silver."

The guy in question turned to look at them, as if he'd heard her words, even though he was too far away for that. He smiled, his eyes sparkling, and Sebastian smelled Fae.

He pushed Sylvia toward Caleb. "We have to get the book and get out of here," he hissed. "This is going to go very bad very soon."

No sooner had he warned her than it did.

The circus was odd.

Theo walked around the circle of stalls, fighting his sense that something was very wrong. Everything looked normal, if a bit tawdry. His senses were a bit overwhelmed by the scent of manure. The signs said they had elephants and there were trailers behind the big tent, like the ones hauled by trucks. Theo had looked around there, initially to see if Niall's suspicions were correct, then had been intrigued by his strong sense of community. The circus people obviously lived in the collection of camper vans that were parked back there, most of which had been adorned or embellished or creatively repaired. The cargo trailers had been converted for livestock, with barred windows, and banners for the circus painted on their sides. They probably made a colorful convoy on the interstate.

Then a pair of security guards had told him that it was a restricted area and escorted him back to the circle of stalls at the front. He thought it curious that they smelled so much like dogs, and wondered if they used dogs to protect the area after the circus closed down at night.

Was this circus the source of his sense that the city had changed? It seemed too small to have that much influence, but his feeling that the shadows were crowded was stronger here.

There was music and blinking lights, a lot of colorful costumes, and kids everywhere. They seemed to be having a good time and he was debating the necessity of staying for the show when he smelled something very wrong.

Blood.

Sorcery.

He turned and saw a woman approaching with an intense guy behind him. The guy was surveying the crowd with obvious suspicion, practically glaring at a blond guy in front of the fortune-teller.

"Caleb!" the woman called and an older security guard glanced toward her. He smiled in recognition, but Theo thought he was wary.

"The book," muttered her intense companion and moved very quickly. He'd crossed the space and seized the guard's sleeve in the blink of an eye. Theo felt his own eyes narrow.

"I don't have it," said the guard.

"One of you does," the quick guy said, his gaze flicking between the security guards. "It's stolen property. Hand it over."

The hackles of the security guards seemed to rise.

"It's safe," said the first one.

"No, it's not," the intense guy said. "Not even close." He urged the woman forward and she put out her hand.

"Please," she said, and Theo realized the security guards had all moved closer to the group.

The ringleader left her ticket counter and eased closer.

A blond teenager slipped behind the tent, heading for the restricted area where Theo had just been.

The blond guy left the fortune-teller and looked up, over the heads of the little cluster of people arguing and Theo spotted an archer in the trees high overhead.

An archer?

The archer lifted his bow, taking careful aim, and Theo shifted shape with a roar to defend the woman. He took flight over the circus and breathed fire at the tree, setting it—and with any luck, the archer—aflame. An arrow shot out of the foliage, and the hand of the woman's companion snapped into the air with that remarkable speed. He winced, and Theo saw that he'd snatched the arrow out of the air. He snapped off the shaft and stuck the arrow head in his pocket.

The security guards had disappeared and there were wolves circling and barking. Something glinted on the ground and Theo saw the woman bend to pick up a book. Her companion swore, then pivoted to run, picking her up as he disappeared like a flash of lightning. The big blond guy followed him, just about as fast.

Chaos reigned in the park, as people screamed and ran. One wolf raised its snout to howl and the eerie sound echoed over the city park. It sounded mournful, especially when the other wolves joined the cry.

Theo shivered as the ringleader cracked her whip, trying to establish order. She shouted for everyone to calm down, but Theo flew after the archer, who was running through the tops of the trees with incredible agility. The park ended though and Theo flew low, intending to fry the archer when he reached the end of the trees.

In the last tree, though, the archer stopped and looked back at Theo. He smiled, and the confidence of his expression startled Theo into holding his fire.

Then he shimmered silver and disappeared in a flash of starlight.

Sylvia had the book.

She held it tightly with both hands, not really caring where Sebastian took her as long as it was safe. He ran faster than she ever could, zipping through the city like quicksilver, and she hoped he had a secure destination. The blond guy followed, almost but not quite as fast as Sebastian.

Then he disappeared.

He appeared again right beneath them two blocks later.

"Fucking magick," Sebastian muttered and kicked at the blond guy. His boot landed in the guy's eye, the force of the blow making him stagger backward. The silver of his aura dimmed a bit, but he recovered more quickly than Sylvia would have liked.

Sebastian was running as if the hounds of hell were after him.

"He's coming again."

"Thank you very much for that update," Sebastian said through his teeth.

"Can you run any faster?"

"I can run more erratically," he said, to her confusion.

"What does that mean?"

"Tell me when he disappears."

"Now," Sylvia said as the guy shimmered and faded to nothing. Sebastian took a hard right, raced down the entry to a subway station, and leaped over the fare turnstiles. He lunged into the tunnel, to the astonishment of the people on the platform, and sped after a departing train. He caught the back end of it and swung them onto it, watching behind them.

"We should be able to catch the 9:16," he

murmured. In the next station, he jumped to another train, headed in another direction, holding Sylvia tightly against his side. "Time?" he asked.

"9:16," she confirmed and he made a little grunt of satisfaction. "Let me guess. You like when subways run on time."

"When they help me lose Fae warriors, yes, I do."

"Fae warriors?"

"That's what the silver light means. It's the light of their realm, following them into this one."

Sylvia blinked. "Where is he?"

"Wherever he thought we were going to be. Fortunately, with pursuit magick, the spellcaster has to decide upon the exact coordinates of his or her destination before disappearing."

"How did he disappear?"

"Technically, he didn't. He slipped into Fae, that parallel realm, but to slip back with any accuracy means choosing in this world before entering that one."

"Do you know a lot about magick?"

"I know enough to get myself into trouble, and to respect it."

"You seem to know enough to get us out of trouble."

"Don't count on that just yet."

In the next station, Sebastian swung onto the platform with enviable grace. There was only one person there, a shabby older man who was suitably startled by their sudden appearance. Sylvia saw him looking into the brown paper bag he carried with new respect and smothered a smile. They were up the stairs and on an abandoned street in no time. Sylvia guessed they were on the west side again, near the piers. She was sure of it when she recognized the street.

"Isn't that the Intrepid Museum ahead?" she asked, not sure why Sebastian would have brought her to a closed military museum on a decommissioned aircraft carrier.

"Yes, but more importantly, the *Growler* is docked beside it."

"The what?"

"A guided missile submarine," he said, pausing then flitting across the last distance. He raced down the dock and Sylvia saw a flicker of silver far behind them.

"We have company," she warned.

"Too late," he said, leaping onto the vessel. He clung to the shadows as the security guard came by, silently picking the lock on the hatch. She didn't think it would be possible but a second later, he opened the hatch silently. He ushered her inside, glancing back and smiling as he gave someone the finger.

Then he jumped in behind her and sealed the hatch behind them.

Something landed on the submarine, then footsteps ran across the top. Sylvia saw a glimmer of silver light around the hatch and feared the blond guy would tear it open.

Then the light faded to nothing.

Sebastian exhaled and leaned against the wall. "Tell me you still have the book."

Sylvia nodded then looked around, knowing her curiosity showed. "A submarine?" she asked. There wasn't a lot of light inside, just security lights, and she was glad. It was harder to tell just how small it was, but even so, her claustrophobia was making her breathe more quickly.

Sebastian nodded. "But more importantly, a perfectly sealed enclosure of steel."

Sylvia could have done without the reminder. She fought against her sense of being trapped, then understood his reference. "The Fae aren't supposed to like iron."

"No 'supposed to' about it. They hate it. It burns them."

"You're supposed to be burned by sunlight."

He strolled down the narrow passageway, peering left and right, as if he hadn't heard her. Of course, he had, but she already guessed that Sebastian wasn't one who would itemize his weaknesses.

Assuming he had any.

He gestured to a room on the right. "Hungry?"

"It's part of a museum. I doubt there's any food."

He leaned in the doorway and smiled. "None that you'd enjoy anyway."

Sylvia realized he was looking at her neck. "When do you need to feast again?"

His eyes seemed to glow. "After all that exercise, I am feeling a little peckish." Sylvia's heart skipped, and she wondered if he was teasing her or serious. He had that little smile as if he might be making a joke, but she wasn't sure. When she didn't reply, he extended his hand. "Better to distract myself with some reading, don't you think?"

Sylvia didn't want to surrender the book. She didn't want Sebastian looking at her like she was dessert either. No doubt he could rip open any door in this place so the only option was to remain awake.

And keep him talking.

She held tightly to the book and stepped past Sebastian, finding a room filled with tables and benches. It was a mess hall, and one big enough that she didn't feel quite as claustrophobic. There was a galley at the end. The space was shadowed and seemed cozy in a strange way. She told herself that it was much bigger than it looked, which was a lie, and that the ceiling was too high to see. Another lie, but if she could believe it a little bit, she could keep from panicking. She didn't want to think about being locked in a steel tube that was partially submerged. She didn't want to think about how many hours it would be until daylight, either.

And what happened then?

She eased onto a bench, the book before herself like a shield. There was a red and black checkerboard on the table in front of her. Sebastian leaned in the doorway, looking lethal and very sexy.

Predatory.

Maybe she should take her chances with the Fae. No, Sebastian had protected her already, and he'd done it more than once. Sylvia chose to trust him. "What happens tomorrow?"

"I'm not psychic."

"But if you can't go out in the sunlight, what happens to me? Can the Fae tolerate sunlight?"

"Of course." He slid onto the bench opposite her, his gaze so intent that she swallowed.

He watched her throat move with an unsettling intensity, then caught his breath and averted his gaze. He drummed his fingers on the table with impatience.

Was he paler than he had been?

"The museum doesn't open until ten," he said. "There's time to make a plan." His gaze collided with hers and she was struck again by how blue his eyes were. They could have been faceted sapphires. "I believe we should leave before dawn."

So he could safely get to wherever he spent his days.

"What about me?"

His smile was slow and sensual, hot enough to make her sizzle all over again. "You could come with me, of course."

She wasn't sure she was up for that. Sylvia averted her gaze, his attention making her aware of both her femininity and her mortality. She still felt his gaze as keenly as a touch.

If she kept him talking, that might distract both

of them. "I'll let you look, if you tell me everything you know about this," she offered.

"If I told you everything, I'd want more than a look in the book in exchange."

Sylvia held up a finger. "Stay out of my dreams."

His smile turned wicked. "But you have interesting dreams," he murmured and Sylvia felt warm all over.

"Three questions," she suggested. "Then you get five minutes to look at the book."

"Fifteen."

"Fifteen," she agreed, wondering if he'd be able to speed-read it all in that much time. "Then another round if we're both agreeable."

"Are you always so studious?"

"Only when my life relies upon it," Sylvia said, which wasn't quite true.

Sebastian's smile faded. "Fair enough," he said and raised a finger. "Question number one."

After the woman fled with one man and the second in hot pursuit, everything quickly returned to normal at the circus.

Or as normal as things could be at a circus like this one.

Theo was thinking about those two men and their scents. Was one a vampire? And the other's scent was odd but unidentifiable to him. Almost like *Slayer*, but not quite. And the *Slayers* were all gone.

The ringleader cracked her whip as if calling

everyone to order. The security guards, who were apparently wolf shifters, shimmered and returned to their human form. The fortune-teller and the clowns began to circulate among the remaining humans, asking how they'd liked the trick. Theo shifted shape and landed high in one of the trees, then jumped down as if he'd been there in his human form all along.

A silver-haired security guard met him at the bottom of the tree. "*Pyr*?" he asked in a soft growl.

Theo nodded, surprised. "How did you know?" And why hadn't Theo known there were wolf shifters in the city? Did their presence explain his strange feeling? Did Erik, leader of the *Pyr*, know there were other shifters in the world? Theo had never heard a mention of them.

"Melissa Smith's specials, of course. You guys are famous." The guard didn't seem to approve of that. "Can you beguile? We could use some help minimizing the damage."

"Sure. What exactly happened here?"

"Fae attack," the wolf shifter said. He lifted a brow. "Vampire rescue. We'll see how that works out." He offered his hand. "I'm Caleb Davison."

Theo shook his hand, liking the other man's firm grip. "Theo Stephens."

"There's got to be more of you," Caleb said.

"And if there are?"

"This isn't the first or the last of the Fae attacks." Caleb pulled a card from his pocket and offered it to Theo. "Come to Bones on Halloween to meet more of the Others. We've got to work together to win this one."

Bones. And the 'Others'. That had to mean more shifters—and more shifters he hadn't known about. Theo eyed the card and the address. He was meeting some of the other *Pyr* in New York for the weekend but could call them early. If there was a battle to be fought, they'd want to be part of it. He definitely wanted to meet these Others.

"If you could do some beguiling, that would be great," Caleb said, indicating the ringleader. "Rosanna is gathering the most skeptical people there."

Emily was right on time for work on Monday morning, which she personally considered to be a miracle. She had a long drive into Philly but the traffic had been particularly light. Maybe everyone was taking the week off for Halloween. She waved to the crew as she walked into the offices, eager to learn what was planned for the week.

Her boss, Maeve O'Neill, was leaning on a desk and checking messages on her phone. She looked sleek and expensive as always, and Emily admired again how polished Maeve was all the time. Her make-up and clothes were always perfect, so she could walk on camera with no delay, and she did everything in four inch heels. She was wearing a black suit with a pencil skirt and a brilliant red silk blouse. Her lipstick matched the blouse and her

dark hair nearly matched the suit. She was a strikingly beautiful woman.

"How was your trip?" she asked with a slight smile.

"It was great," Emily said, putting down her messenger bag. "Nothing like a few days in the big city to make me appreciate home."

"It was your friend's birthday, wasn't it?" Maeve was looking at her phone again. Of course, she wasn't hugely interested—she was too important for that—but Emily was always impressed that Maeve remembered so many details of her employees' lives.

"It was. And we went to that place. It was great."

"What place?"

"You shared the review. A barbeque place called Bones."

Maeve's eyes lit. "Oh, right. I'd forgotten about it. And good?"

Emily nodded agreement. "But stay away from that cocktail they mix called Name Your Poison. That is one fierce drink and I had two. Big mistake." She laughed and Maeve laughed with her.

"Maybe not such a bad way for your friend to celebrate her birthday."

"Oh, she didn't drink one. Not Sylvia Fontaine. She's all about white wine." Emily stuck out her tongue. "I'd rather have water." She shook her head. "The weird thing is that she was seeing auras even before we got a drink."

"Auras?" Maeve asked, her voice sharpening

slightly.

Emily glanced up to find her boss's green eyes glittering with interest. That made her look hungry in a very unsettling way. Emily looked down at her bag, feeling like she'd been caught telling tales out of school. She cleared her throat, making her tone dismissive. "She said they were like animal ghosts behind people. Really weird."

"That is strange. Maybe she started celebrating early." Maeve, to Emily's relief, was focused on her phone again and her tone was distracted.

"That's what I thought. So, where are you going this week?"

"There's a little story in Florida that I've been asked to follow up," Maeve said, tapping her phone. "I'm sending you the details. Maybe you can get a flight this morning for me and the team. I don't think we'll be there long, but then there's something interesting in Nevada I'd like to explore..."

"Good morning!" Bryant called from the doorway. Emily turned to smile at Maeve's cameraman, who was the most cheerful person she'd ever known. He was also really good looking, with his tousle of blond hair and his sparkling blue eyes. He was tall and buff and could seriously wear a pair of jeans—or anything else, for that matter. Not for the first time, Emily regretted just a little bit that she was so happy with Mike.

Bryant grinned at her and winked. "Stay out of trouble in the Big Apple this weekend?" he teased.

"Pretty much."

"That's disappointing." He strolled into the office and perched on a desk. "I've got a present for you, Maeve," he said and she finally looked up from her phone. "I went to this when I was in the city, and it was one sad operation. You'd be doing the world a favor if you did a feature on it and got it shut down."

Maeve's eyes gleamed and he produced a flyer, waving it beneath her nose. *"Circus of Wonders,"* she read, her tone thoughtful. Emily gasped in recognition of the name. "It doesn't look that bad."

"It was terrible." Bryant turned to Emily. "You been there?"

"No, but my friend's new neighbor works there, as a security guard."

"Small world," Bryant said, raising a hand to invite Maeve's opinion.

"We should check it out, after Florida," she said and gave Emily the flyer. "See about making some arrangements for the end of the week."

"You'd better go if you're going to catch that flight," Emily reminded her.

And just like that, everything was back to normal. Maeve grabbed her make-up bag and Bryant loaded up his camera and gear, the two of them comparing notes. Emily booted up her computer, put on her headset and got back to the business of getting Maeve O'Neill, roving reporter, to wherever she needed to go.

The house was quiet when Eithne took the keys to the cellar from the hook beside her fridge. She knew what she had to do, but she was worried about the results. She didn't hurry, just in case something changed and she could avoid this task.

But nothing changed. The air remained charged with peril. Her fears for Sylvia were undiminished. Her awareness of Others only grew stronger.

She unlocked the door at the bottom of the stairs, hesitating on the threshold. The cellar was dark but it was dry. She'd bought the house because of its cellar, nestled in a solid foundation and secure. There was junk in the cellar but that was just for appearances, in case anyone ever managed to get in.

The only thing of importance was the long stone box that was aligned with one long wall. It was under her own apartment, under her own bed, so that she could listen without entering the cellar.

Not a sound came from within the stone box, which was exactly how it should be. Eithne sighed and ran her hands over it, hesitating before she did what she knew she had to do.

It had been so chaotic the last time. She shook her head, hoped for the best, then lifted the stone lid. Most people would have been surprised to see such a slight older woman showing such physical power, but it wasn't force that lifted the lid of the sarcophagus.

It was magick.

Magick sparked from the tips of Eithne's fingers and it sparkled in her hair. It surrounded her with a glow of possibility and it lit the walls of the cellar. It also illuminated the face of the man who was apparently sleeping in the sarcophagus. His breathing was so slow that it was almost non-existent. His pulse was so quiet that it was almost impossible to detect.

He hadn't aged more than a day since she'd enchanted him. She was well aware that she looked older and wondered how he would respond to his first sight of her in over two millennia.

And he was just as handsome as he'd been when she first met him, so many *many* centuries before. His hair was dark and a little long. His features were chiseled perfection—Eithne particularly admired his aquiline nose. His lips were firm but full. He looked like he was smiling, as if his dreams were sweet. She knew he was a good foot taller than her and a lot broader, all muscled strength and grace, just as a dragon shifter should be.

She bent her knee and bowed her head, touching his hand only briefly. His eyelids fluttered, giving her a glimpse of the clear green of his eyes.

"Your majesty," she said softly, for his keen hearing meant there was no need to raise her voice. "It is time to rise."

DRAGON'S KISS
The DragonFate Novels #2

Her kiss could be his doom…

When dragon-shifter Kristofer feels his firestorm ignite, he eagerly follows its spark to his destined mate. To his surprise, the heat leads him to a Valkyrie intent on claiming his soul. Even so, Kristofer has never met a woman as alluring as the fierce warrior before him. Trusting in the firestorm, he must convince her to fight with him instead of against him.

Trading the life of a dragon shifter for that of her sister Valkyrie is an easy choice for Bree…until she meets Kristofer. Experience taught her that dragons are evil, but in him she sees a bold and noble warrior. Finding his confidence as irresistible as his touch, Bree fears she is being tricked into abandoning her sister. But how can she take Kristofer's life when his very presence makes her burn with desire?

When they're compelled to join forces, Kristofer seizes the chance to convince Bree that they're stronger together. Yet as a sinister plan unfolds, an ancient dragon is roused from his slumber. With danger closing in, can Kristofer convince Bree to surrender her immortality for their forbidden love? Or will Bree's distrust of dragons prove justified?

Available Now!

Learn more at http://DragonfireNovels.com

DRAGON'S HEART
The DragonFate Novels #3

Her kiss will rock his world…

Dragon shifter Rhys believes in what he can hold in his talons. A chef with his own restaurant, he is organized, practical, and distrusts surprises. When his firestorm sparks in the realm of Fae, he's sure it's an illusion created by the Dark Queen and a trap. Even though he wants a partner and family again more than anything else, Rhys isn't going to be seduced by a fake destined mate—even if the kiss of that beautiful selkie melts his very soul and is one temptation he can't resist…

Selkie Lila learned long ago that her independence is her most precious possession. But Rhys challenges everything she believes to be true about mortals—he defends her right to choose, even at his own peril, and that's more seductive than Lila wants to admit. Is it just a trick to convince her to bear his son? Or is this *Pyr* warrior as honorable as he appears to be?

When an ancient and evil dragon prince joins forces with the Dark Queen to eliminate both the *Pyr* and the selkies, Rhys and Lila must work together to save their kinds—and each other. When they plunge into unknown realms with only each other to rely upon, will their combined abilities be enough to triumph— or will they have to surrender more for their unborn son and the chance of a future together?

Available Now!

Learn more at http://DragonfireNovels.com

ABOUT THE AUTHOR

Deborah Cooke sold her first book in 1992, a medieval romance called Romance of the Rose published under her pseudonym Claire Delacroix. Since then, she has published over fifty novels in a wide variety of sub-genres, including historical romance, contemporary romance, and paranormal romance. She has published under the names Claire Delacroix, Claire Cross and Deborah Cooke. **The Beauty**, part of her successful Bride Quest series of historical romances, was her first title to land on the *New York Times* List of Bestselling Books. Her books routinely appear on other bestseller lists and have won numerous awards. In 2009, she was the writer-in-residence at the Toronto Public Library, the first time the library has hosted a residency focused on the romance genre. In 2012, she was honored to receive the Romance Writers of America's Mentor of the Year Award.

Currently, she writes paranormal romances and contemporary romances as Deborah Cooke. She also writes historical romances as Claire Delacroix. Deborah lives in Canada with her husband and family, as well as far too many unfinished knitting projects.

To learn more about her books, visit her websites:
http://deborahcooke.com
http://dragonfirenovels.com
http://dragonsofincendium.com
http://delacroix.net